DISCARD

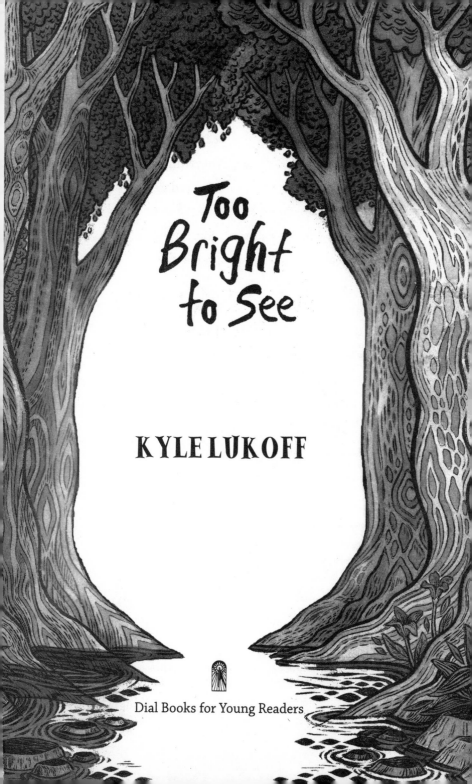

Too Bright to See

KYLE LUKOFF

Dial Books for Young Readers

DIAL BOOKS FOR YOUNG READERS
An imprint of Penguin Random House LLC, New York

First published in the United States of America by Dial Books for Young Readers,
an imprint of Penguin Random House LLC, 2021

Visit us online at penguinrandomhouse.com.

Library of Congress Control Number: 2021936337

Printed in the United States of America
ISBN 9780593111154

10 9 8 7 6 5 4 3 2

Design by Cerise Steel
Text set in Chaparral Pro

For all the students who came through my library at Corlears School, 2012–2020. This book is because of you.

Prologue

It's strange living in our old house, now that Uncle Roderick is dead.

I already know my house is haunted. It's always been haunted. That hasn't changed. We avoid the freezing cold spot in the corner of the living room because someone probably died there. Windows slam themselves open or shut on the stillest days. So do doors, and these doors are heavy. For a long time I thought it was normal to sense someone standing behind you, or next to you, and not be able to see them. For invisible hands to brush past your hair, your clothes.

And it looks haunted: wooden, unpainted, weathered with time. There's an elaborately carved front door, peaked roofs jutting out in all directions, tall windows with shapes flickering behind them. The porch wraps around front to back with rocking chairs that sometimes rock on their own. We're out in the middle of nowhere, and at nighttime there's moonlight and starlight and nothing else. When I was in kindergarten I checked a book out of the library because the house on the front cover looked like a photograph of my home. Uncle Roderick tried reading it to me that night, my head resting on his chest, his arm tucked beneath my shoulders. We always read together before bed. He had to stop after the first chapter because it was a collection of scary stories; he believed that dreams were important, and he didn't want to give me bad ones.

But now this old house seems haunted in a different way. A way that's both more boring and more frightening. There's a half-empty jar of okra Uncle Roderick picked and pickled that he'll never finish eating, and Mom and I both hate okra. His winter boots are jammed in the closet. He always put off wearing them for as long as possible, saying they made him look like a lumberjack, but now he'll never need them again. He subscribed to magazines, the *New Yorker*, *National Geographic*, and they'll keep being addressed to him until we tell them to stop. Until they take his name off the list. Forever.

I prefer the ghosts.

one

The moment he dies, I know. It's the middle of the night. My eyes open, and I grip the mattress with both hands. I'm suddenly, irrationally convinced that my bed is toppling over. Like it's unbalanced, perched precariously on the top of a mountain and about to come crashing down. Or like it's teetering on the edge of a black hole, with nothing familiar on the other side.

Uncle Roderick's room is at the top of the stairs. Mom's is at the end of the hall. For eleven years I've fallen asleep snug in the middle, their warmth and weight keeping me grounded from both sides. Even these past couple months, when he's been in the hospital and then the hospice, I could still feel him there, keeping me safe at the top of the stairs. But now I know my uncle is gone.

The stairs creak, sharp and loud. That doesn't mean anything. They creak all the time. "The house is settling" is what Mom says, and sometimes it might be a harmless ghost. But now I hear the groan of a foot on a step. And then another. It's like the sound of someone slowly moving up our wide staircase, someone with a heavy tread.

It's mid-June, and hot, and I'm lying under a sheet with a fan blowing warm air around the room. I pull the sheet up to my chin, wishing for the weight of a comforter to press me into the mattress, something to hide under.

The creaks stop at the top, right in front of Uncle Roderick's bedroom door. I hold my breath and strain my ears. I can't hear anything, but it doesn't sound like no one's there. It sounds like someone being silent. I only exhale when the creaks descend the stairs, as slowly as they came.

Uncle Roderick always told me that passing spirits and lingering presences are a normal part of living in a house almost as old as the dirt it sits on. Mom says that the creepy things I sense or feel or hear are just part of an active imagination, and that Uncle Roderick shouldn't encourage it, that ghosts aren't real.

I only occasionally believe my mom: When the sun is bright and I can explain away strange hands touching my neck or a mysteriously slammed-shut door as stray gusts of wind in a drafty old building.

I believe my uncle now, surely and suddenly. But I don't want to. "There's no one on the stairs," I tell myself, wanting it to be true, still holding on to the mattress for dear life. "There's no one on the stairs. There's no one on the stairs. There's no one on the stairs." The rhythm pounds through my brain, repeating itself over and over, crowding out every other thought that also must be true. I manage to fall asleep by curling up into a ball, my back turned toward the half of the room that echoes the new emptiness in my chest.

I wake up again a few hours later because the phone rings. I feel grounded now. Not in a free fall, not hurtling through space. But there's an empty room inside my chest.

Mom's voice struggles through the wall. None of the words are clear, but if I didn't know about Uncle Roderick already, I would know now from her tone, the rise and fall of sentences. She comes into my bedroom a few minutes later and I sit up.

She holds me and cries. I've seen my mother cry before, but it's never been my job to comfort her. It's always been Uncle Roderick's job. But her brother's not here, and I am. I hold her tight, and breathe as shallowly as possible until her sobs subside. I should have cried that first day, almost a year ago, when Uncle Roderick came home from the doctor with bad news, but I couldn't. I remember a rushing sound filling my ears, drowning out the details, my brain refusing to take in anything beyond one main truth. Something too big to touch, with no details to snag on. I told myself I'd only cry once he was gone. But that day has come and I've got nothing. No tears, and no anything else. There's sadness, but it's whirling around outside of me. Like a hurricane of grief, and I'm the dry, unmoving eye.

"He loved you very much, you know," Mom says, after

a bit. She lets go, sits up straight, palms the tears off her cheeks. I wish I had a tissue to offer her.

"I know he did," I say. And I do. But it doesn't help. Mom hugs me once more, then says she has to make some phone calls. I stare across my room, sunlight streaming through the tall window with rippled glass, and wonder what happens after this.

two

Mom and Uncle Roderick and I rattled around our house like peas in an oversized pod. Sometimes we would have houseguests from New York City or Burlington or Montreal, filling it up with noise and laughter and memories. But the three of us could fill it up just as well.

Tonight the house is full of people and memories, but not much laughter. Family friends have come from all over. But not many people from our little pocket of Vermont show up. We moved here when I was a baby, and old Vermonters don't acknowledge you until there's "six in the ground." Six dead people, they mean, in a row, stretching back through the years. Well, we've got our first.

But Uncle Roderick isn't even in the ground. Not really. He didn't want a funeral, he said, or a burial. *Just sprinkle my ashes on the land,* he told us toward the end. We did, putting handfuls in the creek, the woods, the garden, everywhere.

Mom says that everyone deserves a chance to say goodbye. I wish they could say goodbye somewhere else. The house has never been this full before, and I can't go hide with Uncle Roderick in his room. I have to wear this dress that makes me look like Samantha from the American Girl books. It's rumpled from being at the bottom of my closet for months, and Uncle Roderick usually took care of the ironing.

People pat me on the shoulder or hug me, and since I'm the one with a dead uncle it's okay that I don't hug back. My dress is like a force field; it blocks out the pressure of their hands or arms around me, which is good because if I actually feel anyone touch me I'll break apart into smithereens. In between I focus on tightening my ponytail and tugging at the wrinkles in my dress. It's too small for me, and if I hunch forward the material pulls across my back, keeping me a gasp away from a full breath.

Conversations pause if I walk by them, but tucked into a corner of the living room I catch snatches here and there.

"Awfully young, he was only thirty-two, right?"

"It's so sad, especially since Sabrina's husband died right after she gave birth. A car accident, if I'm remembering correctly."

"No, they don't have anyone else. This place started out as a vacation home, and it's been in their family for a while, but no one else is left."

One of Uncle Roderick's ex-boyfriends is across the room, down from Portland. I think his name is Tobias. He's tall and thin, like Uncle Roderick, but with a shaved head and a beard. He was nice, but had wanted kids, and my uncle decided that I was enough kid for him, so they broke up but stayed friends. Tobias catches my eye and gives me a small, sad smile. I turn up the corners of my mouth in what might be a smile, and skitter away before he can come over to shake my hand or hug me or pay whatever respects he has.

I duck into the kitchen but catch my dress on the doorframe. I reach down to tug it away, from a nail or whatever. It's not stuck on anything, but there's a rip that I don't think was there before. Oh well, I'm getting too big for it anyway.

No one else is in the kitchen. There are dishes cluttered on the wide wooden counter, crusted with food, so I dump them in the sink and turn on the faucet. I've always begged Mom for a dishwasher, especially since I only just got tall enough to reach the bottom of the huge sink, but right now scrubbing at dishes in hot soapy water quiets the jangling in my brain. I start planning out what I need to pack for summer camp, and have gotten into a rhythm of washing and rinsing when I look up at the window behind the sink.

A strange face stares back at me, darkly reflected in the glass.

I yelp, jump back, and a glass slips out of my hand and crashes onto the kitchen floor. A second later the kitchen door swings open.

"You okay, Bug?" a voice calls out. Mo. My best, or oldest, or only friend. She and her mom showed up a while ago, but I haven't said hi yet.

The dress is still pulling on my back and shoulders. "Fine," I say. I can't figure out how to get my mouth to say more than that. I grab at a broom and dustpan to hide my shaking hands.

This happens a lot. I'll be minding my own business, in the bathroom or kitchen or wherever, and catch a glimpse of something in the mirror that isn't me. Not a blood-dripping evil face, or anything obviously supernatural. Just a face that isn't quite mine. Almost mine. But different enough that it gives me a shock every time. Another part of living in a haunted house, I guess. Except it doesn't happen only when I'm at home.

Mo always makes me swear that she won't get attacked by ghosts when she spends the night at my house. I always promise, but that's because ghosts don't attack people. Don't notice people, even. They're in their own world, whatever that is, and we're in this one. The only times we overlap are like how if you look into a bright light for too long you see it even after you look away, even when you close your eyes. It's not in front of you, but it still leaves an impression.

Mo has never even seen one of those. She's scared of coming across a tall woman in a bloodstained wedding gown, or a pale little boy with a bad smile, but doesn't notice when her hair is caught in a nonexistent breeze or a room's mood shifts while it remembers something. I don't tell her when it happens, because Mo's the only person who's willing to sleep over in the first place.

I finish sweeping and lean back against the kitchen island. Mo hops onto it next to me. I can tell she's struggling to come up with something to say. She always has something to say, and right now I don't want to listen, but it's nice, or something, of her to try.

"Where did that dress come from?" she asks finally. "I've never seen it before."

It's better than asking how I am doing. There's no good answer. I wonder if she knows better than to ask that, or if she's actually curious about the dress. I'd rather not talk about anything, just moving my mouth feels hard, but I don't want Mo to start chattering away, which is what she usually does if I don't keep up my end of a conversation.

"I don't remember. It's old." My voice surprises me. It sounds normal. "Mom said I might need a dress for some occasion. I look like my old Samantha doll."

"Ha, yeah, you do. I still have my Felicity somewhere. Remember when we would make up whole stories with them? Yours always involved pirates or kidnappings or something. I always wanted to take them to balls. And then we would compromise! Pirate ball or glamorous kidnapped princess."

I just nod, and look down at the puffy skirt. It really does look more like a costume than a dress. Mo looks like she's going to a funeral instead of our house, in a smooth dark skirt and matching top. Her bright red hair is in a tight braid, not loose and frizzy like normal. She's a few months younger than me, but she looks almost like an adult today. Almost like a woman. I just look like a doll. Quiet, stiff, and blinking.

"We have to go," she says after a minute of silence. "I just came in to say goodbye. I'll see you soon, though. And . . . um, I'm so sorry." She leans in to hug me, and I manage to lift my arms and squeeze her back for a second, before it becomes too much. She's always been the type to put her arms around her other friends, play with their hair, a casual affection that has always seemed impossible to me. I'm never sure how bodies are supposed to interact. I feel like I'm hugging a scarecrow. Or more that I'm a scarecrow being hugged. Mo gives me an awkward pat on the back before pushing her shoulder against the swinging kitchen door. Her skirt doesn't catch on anything.

I go back to the sink and start washing dishes again. The kitchen has always been my favorite room in the house. It's where I watched Uncle Roderick bake cookies and can vegetables, experiment with new recipes. And it's kind in here. Safe. I imagine what I must look like, a girl with long hair pulled back, a torn dress, scrubbing away like a servant girl in a royal palace, and thinking about that girl and imagining her life keeps me distracted from what is actually happening. The soapy water has gone cold, and I finish up without looking at the window again.

three

Some guests stay for a few days after the memorial. I make myself useful, dodging questions about how I'm holding up by doing endless loads of dishes and laundry. I pretend to be a character in a book, sometimes an abused but brilliant servant girl, sometimes a spy at a seedy hotel, sometimes a princess mistaken for a commoner. It's fun. Kind of. It's something I've always done. Girls in books always seem more real than real life, and making believe that I'm in a story keeps my mind off of what I really am, which isn't much.

It takes a couple days, but finally everyone goes back to where they live. Big cities, for most of them. I was born in Brooklyn, but Mom moved us here when I was only a few months old. After my dad died she says she didn't know how to stop one life (married, no kids) and start a new one (widowed, kid) without going all the way. Without making another huge change.

Uncle Roderick came with her. "I never thought it was going to be permanent," he told me last year, while we were picking blueberries. He'd use them in a pie later, but I was eating mine right off the bush. "We would vacation up here when we were kids, but neither of us had any reason to stay in Vermont. I thought we'd spend a couple years, she'd heal from the loss of your dad, and then we'd go back. But kids root you to a place. It's like we grew down into this earth, instead of growing up from it."

The biggest city I've been to is Burlington, on a school field trip. I learned that Burlington is the smallest biggest— the biggest city in the state, and the smallest city with that distinction. It felt huge to me, people everywhere I looked, stores on top of stores on top of stores. Uncle Roderick talked about bringing me to New York, but we never made it. I don't think I'll ever visit now.

It's morning, the house is empty of everyone except Mom and me, and I'm staring at Uncle Roderick's carved wooden tea cabinet, perched below the spice rack. Dying for a cuppa, like they say in old books from England. I don't know any other eleven-year-olds who drink tea, but Uncle Roderick started making it for me, mostly honey and milk, once I graduated from sippy cups. I know there's a half-full drawer of jasmine in there, and I miss the weight of a heavy mug warming my hands. The comfort of sipping at some-thing hot and sweet. But I can't bring myself to boil water, ease open the rickety drawer, measure leaves into a tea ball, steep it properly. Too many steps.

I pour myself a glass of juice instead and fix a bowl of cereal. Mom shuffles in, still wearing her robe, looking like she hasn't slept for weeks.

"Thank you for being so helpful these past few days, sweetheart," she says, her voice thick with sleep or grief or both. "You'd make a great scullery maid."

"I know," I mumble. My throat closes around any other words. Normally we'd launch into some conversation about what chores you wouldn't want to do in a medieval castle, or I'd go into some dramatic monologue about working my fingers to the bone, but there isn't any laughter in me. And it wouldn't be the same without Uncle Roderick joining in, with a terrible attempt at an English accent or pretending to be better than me because he's a chambermaid. I stir my spoon around the bowl, and Mom slips out to get the newspaper from the porch. There's not much laughter in her either, and I know she only tried for me.

When she comes back she tosses the comics page down on the counter in front of me and makes herself some coffee. She's never been much of a tea drinker, and I'm grateful for that.

I stare at the comics, not actually reading them. Smiling seems like it would hurt, like clay has dried on my cheeks and a twitch of my lips would crack it off. A prickling at the back of my eyes makes me look up. Mom has the paper spread out in front of her, but she's looking at me like she has more bad news. She swallows hard when I meet her gaze. There are new lines etched around the corners of her mouth, and her eyes are red.

"I know we planned on sending you to camp again in July," she begins softly, and I want to tell her to stop, I know where this is going. But she has that sad half smile on her face that I've seen a lot this past year, so I let her keep going. Mom and Uncle Roderick look so much alike, with shaggy, dirty-blond hair, green eyes, and pointy chins. My skin tans, while their paler skin burns. I have bluer eyes, a bigger nose, dark hair. My dad had dark hair. I keep mine long because it never needs cutting that way. I grab the base of my ponytail and squeeze, the pull on my scalp helping a little.

"Your uncle's insurance covered a lot of his medical bills, but that last place he was in, the hospice, was very expensive. I don't want you to worry; we're not going to starve, but I'm afraid there isn't much extra cash lying around. I promise I'll do everything I can to help you have a fun summer, but camp is out of the question this year. Hopefully next year will be different. I'm so sorry, Bug."

At camp we sleep in a hayloft and gather eggs for breakfast. We play endless games of capture the flag and hide-and-seek, go on midnight walks, canoe in the lake, everything. I'm not great at making friends, but something about the comfortingly consistent bad food, whole-day games of tag, the rainy days when we climb the rock wall in the gym, brings us all together in a way that school can't. Kids come from all over New England, and it's the only time in the year where I feel part of a larger group. I've gone every July since I was six, and stayed for the entire month the past two years. I loved Uncle Roderick, and I loved camp. Now I don't have either.

"It's okay," I say. It isn't, but it is. I should have guessed, after going with Mom to visit Uncle Roderick in the hospital. All those treatments and medicines couldn't have been cheap, and he hadn't worked for a long time, not since he got really sick. Mom has always been honest with me, and talking about money is part of that. I can't whine about missing camp when I understand why. Besides, if I show Mom how upset I am it will only make her feel worse, which won't make anything better. The cereal in my bowl is completely soggy now. There's no way I can finish it. I had only eaten one spoonful anyway. I shove aside my barely touched breakfast and unread comics, and tell Mom that I'm going outside.

She pulls me into her arms as I walk past her, holding me tight. I don't want to be hugged right now, but I know that this hug is for her, that I have to show her that I'm not mad, so I squeeze her until she lets go. Only then do I take a deep breath. It's a beautiful day.

We own a lot of the land around my house. The backyard

is a big grassy field, and beyond that is a patch of woods I've explored ever since I could walk. A creek runs through the woods, and I can spend entire days reading on a boulder near the water or splashing around trying to catch minnows. Uncle Roderick would walk through the woods with me and tell stories of the gnomes and fairies hiding just out of sight, or point out edible plants and poisonous berries. We would pack a picnic lunch and find shapes in the clouds, sit quiet and still and wait for snakes and squirrels to come out around us. It never felt lonely. He would sometimes joke about the big-city life he left behind, glamorous and loud and bright, but he loved filling our big house with restored antiques and chopping wood for winter fires.

My bike is stashed under the porch. I pull it out, brush a spider off the handlebar, and climb on. I pedal away from my house, trying to get up enough speed to catch the wind between my teeth. Then I remember Uncle Roderick teaching me how to ride, putting bandages on my knees and elbows when I fell. I remember following him into town on crisp fall days to visit the farmer's market. I remember him showing me how to change the tire, our hands greasy and black and smelling like rubber and the earth. Something blunt and unstoppable tries to push its way up from my stomach into my throat and behind my eyes. I brake sharply, jump off, and walk back home, leaving my bike sprawled on the side of the dirt road, one wheel still spinning forlornly.

***

I go to bed early that night. Too sad to stay awake. I'm fast asleep until all at once I'm not. It's like the night he died all over again, except instead of a sudden *lack,* a cold nothing where there was once a warm someone, now there's . . . something else. My eyes are still shut tight, but someone is in my room. "Her eyes were shut tight," I say in my head like a narrator, wondering what a girl in a book would do. "She knew it was just her imagination." I try opening them, just barely, and peeking through my eyelashes, but it's so dark. Dark enough that if I open my eyes a little more I'll still be safe. I hope. I squint them open a crack more. And see it.

It? Him? Her? A tall, thin, dark shape looming in front of my closed door. Is it a shadow? Is it moving?

I'm silent. I'm so, so silent. It can't know I'm awake. I'm not even breathing. And then I realize that I've stopped breathing. Sleep breaths are long and slow and steady and it knows I'm awake now. I see it, him, move toward me, and quick as anything I flip on the light next to my bed. I don't know if I want to see, but light will help no matter what.

And nothing's there.

It's not the first time I've been scared in my house, at night. But it's the first time I can't scream and know that my uncle will come running.

When I was very little I had a lot of nightmares. Mom

doesn't wake up for anything, but Uncle Roderick would be by my side right away, talking me through it. He'd ask what I thought it meant, if it represented something I was afraid of in real life, what the dream was trying to tell me. And in discussing, it would fade from memory, completely forgotten in the morning.

I want to call for him now and know that he would come in, sit on the side of my bed, and tell me that ghosts are nothing to be afraid of. That they don't even know we're here, that we're not even in the same world.

But he's resting now. At peace. And I can't help but think that this one felt different. It wasn't in another world. It knew I was there, and it knew I was awake. But I don't know what it wanted, and I don't know why it left.

After that I can only sleep in fits and starts, but by morning I've almost managed to convince myself that it was only a dream. And even if it wasn't a dream—even if there was something, some spirit in my room, it wasn't really all that different from the wandering ghosts that are always whooshing around my house. They've never even paid attention to me. They've never hurt me before.

four

Mo called after breakfast to ask if she could spend the night, so I'm waiting on the front porch with Uncle Roderick's worn collection of Edgar Allan Poe stories. I haven't made it to the library in a while, and he used to read this book to me on cold winter evenings. I want to hear his voice again, a little bit, in today's heat.

A shout comes from down the road and I look up to see Mo struggling her way toward my house. She must have found my bicycle by the side of the road, because she's walking it down the driveway with one hand, guiding hers with the other. Her sleeping bag is squished under one arm, and some heavy-looking shopping bags are looped over the handlebars.

Well, "driveway" is what we call this stretch, even though it's just a dirt road that runs up to my house, which you turn onto from another, slightly bigger gravel road. It only takes twenty minutes to bike between our houses, and we've been doing it regularly for years. I put down my book and launch over the porch railing to help her up the driveway.

"Hey Bug," she calls. "Seen any new ghosts?"

"Just the old ones," I say. She asks that every time she comes to my house, and I always give her the same answer. Last night unfolds in my mind and I suddenly wonder if I'm telling the truth, then shake my head quickly to one side, to knock that thought out of my brain.

Mo unslings the shopping bags and I wheel my bike back under the porch. It's a little dented, grubby, a word for it might be "battered." I like it that way, like something belonging to a scrappy, adventurous youth in some old-timey detective novel. Mo just got a new bike. It was definitely expensive, sleek and rose-gold and it looks just like her, somehow, if a bike could resemble a person. Her old bike had Hello Kitty all over it and neither one of us is into Hello Kitty, so she covered them all up with patches of duct tape a long time ago. I thought it looked cool, but she said she outgrew it, and I don't think she meant by getting taller.

"Thanks for bringing it back," I tell her. Saying that I suddenly got too sad to pedal would lead to a whole conversation I don't want to have, with sighs and sympathetic looks, so "I . . . got a foot cramp earlier," I lie. "Was about to go get it. But thanks."

"No prob. Um, I don't know if you want to talk about it, or whatever," she begins, bringing her bike up onto the porch. I hold my breath against the rising sharpness in my chest. "But your uncle was the best. I'm sorry."

"Yeah," I say tightly, before she can launch into some

memory she has of him. I feel like I'm wearing that old dress again, pulling my rib cage close. "Thanks." The door creaks open wide as soon as we step onto the porch. Mo jumps back and eyes it warily.

"No new ghosts," I tell her, again. I hope I'm right.

"Okay," she says. "But you go in first."

Mo and I didn't get along when we were little, but over the past few years we've slowly figured it out. We didn't have much of a choice. Our moms started a business together when we were toddlers, so we grew up with each other. We definitely wouldn't have been friends if we weren't forced into it, but I'm glad it happened. Most of the time. Now we say we're best friends, and it's true enough, even though memories of when we didn't like each other are always shifting beneath the surface.

All of our other friends were her friends first. Sometimes she invites me to a sleepover at someone else's house, or someone's mom will drive three or four of us to the mall an hour away. Otherwise I play by myself, or with Mo. Or with Uncle Roderick, but I don't want my mind to go there now.

We unroll our sleeping bags in the living room like always. Mo claims the first floor of my house feels less haunted than the second floor, and she won't set foot in the cellar. I don't blame her.

"Hi, Mo," says Mom, coming in through the dining room. "Do you know if your mom got the last shipment of card stock?"

"Not yet," says Mo. "Also, she says she hasn't found a good deal on envelopes, and you should call her to talk about finding a new vendor."

"Not a problem," Mom says. Her tone is light, but something tighter flashes across her face. It's gone before I can blink. "Will you girls be eating dinner with me," she asks, "or should I be a terrible *in loco parentis* and let you eat popcorn and ice cream all night?"

There are enough leftovers from the memorial to last for weeks, and I don't want to abandon Mom yet. "We'll eat with you," I say, and Mo nods in agreement.

Usually when Mo and I spend time with our moms we come up with new card ideas together. After my dad died, Mom says that she got frustrated with all the stupid condolence cards people sent, all sunsets and flowery messages about better places and how everything happens for a reason. She started designing her own cards that were sarcastic and funny but also still sad, and started bringing them into little stationery shops around the area. Mo's mom had experience running a mail-order business, and even though her husband's job meant that she didn't need to work anymore, soon the two of them had a whole line of greeting cards in stores across the country. We're not rich, but—as Mom always tells me—we have everything that we need, and some of what we want.

But tonight none of us feel like talking about clever

responses to sad things. Mo and Mom argue about some YouTuber that I've never heard of. Their laughs float up to the ceiling, sounding hollow and far away, and I tune it out. One tiny bite of potato salad. One leaf of kale salad. One half of a half of a meatball. Everything tastes like nothing. A huge mirror hangs on the wall across from me and I avoid looking at it, pushing my food around instead. When I glance up at Mom, her plate is still as full as mine.

"I just don't understand why you would want to watch someone play a game on the Internet when you could just . . . play that game on the Internet yourself," she's saying. "I played video games for hours when I was your age, but at least I was the one playing them."

"Oh come *on*, Sabrina, didn't you ever, like, watch people play? Like if there was a boy that you liked, and he invited you over to watch him play a video game. You did that, right?"

Mom smirks. "What, exactly, do you know about what boys do when they invite you over?" I'm wondering the same thing. Does she suddenly know what dates are like? As far as I know she's never even held a boy's hand.

Mo flushes, just a little. "I mean, not much, but I've heard that that's a thing people used to do. Or still do. Right?"

"Well, maybe," Mom relents. "Sometimes. But that's different—at least we were in the same physical space!"

"I'm just saying, there's something about watching a

game being played live. You don't have to join in to enjoy it. And there's, like, live commenting, chatting with people who are also watching, that sort of thing. It's not so different from actually sitting with your friends and watching them."

Mom turns to me. "What do you think, Bug? Are you team real world or team Internet?"

I freeze. Mo knows I never want to watch YouTube videos with her, but she might get frustrated if I side with Mom. "Uh . . ." I stall.

Surprisingly, Mo comes to my rescue. "Oh, she's team dead trees. Bug just wants to read, you know that. Has a teacher ever assigned a book you haven't already read?"

I grudgingly shake my head, and Mom laughs. It's nice to hear her laugh, but I wish it had come from something I said. A voice whispers to me that Mo is being a better daughter than me, and it forces me to my feet, forces a lightness in my voice.

"Team dead trees all the way!" I exclaim. "Do you want us to clean up?"

Mom crumples her napkin and drops it onto her plate, as if she's trying to hide how much she didn't eat. "Thanks, love, but I'll take care of it. You two should go watch a movie or something. Mo, thank you for coming over."

"No problem," says Mo. "Um, also, could you start calling me Moira?"

Mom pauses in stacking the dishes and seems about to ask a question, but nods instead. "Of course, Moira. Let me know if you girls need anything."

We go into the living room and I plop down on the couch. "'Moira'?" I ask. No one calls her that, ever.

"We're starting middle school soon, and Mo is a little-kid name. You might want to do the same, *Bug*." I twitch. I hate the name on my birth certificate and never use it. I imagine starting school, introducing myself as—

The lights flicker for a second. Mo jumps, stares balefully at the filigreed-metal lamp, and grabs one of the shopping bags she brought with her. Usually they're full of snacks and DVDs, but when she dumps the bag upside down, jars of nail polish and tubes of lip gloss scatter across the floor, along with other shiny plastic things I don't recognize. The second bag is full of brushes and combs and hair products.

We used to play makeover when we were younger, smearing whatever odds and ends we could scavenge from her mom's stash or Uncle Roderick's collection over each other's faces to see who could look the funniest. I have a sinking suspicion that that isn't Mo's—*Moira's*—plan for tonight.

"What's all this for?" I ask. I tug at my ponytail, hard, then let go, and prickles run up and down my spine, like someone is sitting right behind me. I try not to shudder—if Moira notices anything ghostly she might go home early.

Whatever she wants to do right now is better than being alone.

"Like I said, we're starting middle school." Moira sorts through the pile, putting the nail polish and everything in some kind of order. These are all brand-new, unopened and in bright packaging. She must have gone shopping.

"So?" I ask. "Is there some law saying that you have to cover your face in gunk before you walk through the front door?"

Moira laughs, but I don't think she thought it was funny. "There's no law. But first impressions matter! I heard that all the girls at Maplewood wear makeup and stuff. Well, not all of them, but most of them. Definitely all the popular ones. You want to make a fresh start, right?"

So that's why she's going by her full name. "It's going to be all the same people we know already, they got their first impression of us when we were five. How fresh do you think this start is going to be?" I can't imagine that starting middle school magically erases your memories of what someone looked like three months ago.

"That's not true, there will be kids from a lot of other schools bused in. And sometimes people change over the summer. Come on, do you want middle school to be exactly the same as the past seven years? I definitely do not."

Maybe she has a point. Do I really want middle school to be just like elementary school? No one bullied me, exactly, but I also didn't have any other good friends. I had a reputation for being a teacher's pet, which wasn't fair. I never tried to get teachers to like me, I was just quiet and focused on my work because it was interesting enough, most of the time. And getting good grades just felt like playing a game, and winning. But I didn't bother to explain that, ever, because I knew it wouldn't help. If Mo didn't sit with me at lunch I would find a corner and eat by myself, reading a book. She'd sometimes invite me to sit with her at a more populated table, but I always refused. And I'll bet she was relieved. Even when I tried to follow along with the more popular girls I was always one step out of line, whereas Mo seemed to crack the grade-school girl code without even trying.

Like two years ago, Mo's grandmother gave her a stuffed skunk for Christmas. A babyish gift for a fourth grader, but Mo thought it was cute, and started bringing it with her to school. The next day another girl brought in a stuffed bunny. The day after, most of the class, even the boys, had brought in stuffed animals from home. Our teacher said we could keep them on our desks if they weren't distracting, so the next day I brought one in too. Except instead of an animal, mine was a fuzzy representation of the bubonic plague. I don't know why, Mom picked it up in a kooky shop in a tourist town and I thought it was funny.

No one else thought so, and a rumor spread that if you sat next to me you'd get some awful disease. Everyone was used to calling me Bug, but suddenly that became a joke,

"Bug has bugs," that sort of thing. Mo didn't join in, but she also didn't make any big speeches about why it was cool to be different—no matter what teachers and books say, that would have been embarrassing for both of us. The next day I brought in a squirrel puppet, but the fad was over by then and no one but Mo would sit next to me for weeks. That's the only time in my life I considered going by my real name.

"Pick a color," Moira encourages. "I'll do your nails." I grab a bottle at random, "Strawberrylicious," according to the label, and hand it to her. It can't hurt to practice, I guess.

The smell of nail polish uncurls under my nose as she starts carefully painting my fingernails. It reminds me of those playdates when we were little kids. Back then, the colors weren't Strawberrylicious. We would paint each nail a different shade of blue, or alternate Christmas colors, or a rainbow. Most of the time it looked like we dipped our entire fingertips into the bottle. This precise, methodical application is new.

"You might want to ask your mom to take you shopping," she says, brow furrowed as she focuses on each nail. "You don't want to start the school year in the same old clothes, right?"

I haven't really thought about it. "I haven't really thought about it," I say.

"Well, if you want I could go with and help you pick out some cute new outfits," she says. "You can have your own style, of course, but I don't know if it's a good idea to keep dressing like a boy."

She says that like it's obvious, but this is news to me. I look down at my cutoff jean shorts and baggy T-shirt. "Do I dress like a boy?" I ask. "I'm not trying to. I just dress like . . . I don't know. I just wear whatever."

Mo laughs a little. "There are also plenty of boys who dress better than you. We could get you a pink bow tie if you want, that could work. Come on, it'll be fun." She's not trying to be mean, I don't think, but there's no nice way to tell someone that they're doing something wrong. Which, apparently, I am.

I don't know what to say. I don't want to have a style. Suddenly my old shirt and shorts feel like they're sticking to me. But Mo is still painting my nails. My stomach starts to race, and my heart matches it thrum for thrum. Mo doesn't seem to notice anything wrong, and releases my hands.

"Voila!" she exclaims, in a bad French accent. "A bee-YOU-tiful manicure for ze bee-YOU-tiful young lady. And now, ze face." I close my eyes and force myself to sit still as she starts messing with my face. This is nothing like the smeary paint jobs I remember. I wonder if she's been practicing, or if this is another thing she suddenly understands that I don't.

Her fingers are soft and light, moving delicately from my

eyes to my cheeks to my lips, and I keep my breathing shallow and steady. The queasiness in my stomach turns into something light and tingly. I love having my hair played with, even though I always keep it pulled back in a ponytail, and this is just as soothing. I've read scenes in novels where characters do this kind of thing, and it's always peaceful, and friendly, and eventually transformative. Maybe this whole middle-school-girl thing won't be so bad.

After not long enough, Mo—Moira—puts her hands down and declares me "Feeneeshed." She comes with me to the dining room so we can admire her masterpiece together.

She makes me close my eyes until I'm positioned in front of the mirror.

"Three . . . two . . . one . . . open!"

I open my eyes, and scream.

Moira jumps a mile. "What? What is it?"

My heart's leaped out of my throat but I manage to croak, "Nothing. Surprised. It's okay." I've gotten used to not always recognizing my face in the mirrors of my strange house, but whoever is peering back at me is no one I have ever seen before.

I swallow my heart a little and look at the reflection—*my* reflection—more closely. She's a stranger, but a nice-looking one. I can see my face under hers, but it's like staring at my identical twin, if my identical twin were a pretty-ish girl. My stomach roils again, a stew of surprise and shame and curiosity. I never knew that I could look like that, and I'm not sure how I feel about it. When girls in books or movies get makeovers, they're thrilled with what they see in the mirror. I wonder if that only happens in fiction, or if it's normal to act like you've seen a ghost.

Moira looks at my face in the mirror more critically and I'm suddenly dizzy. This new face is even stranger when I think about it through her eyes. But Moira seems business-like rather than shaken. "Next time I'd use less blush and a darker eye shadow. But it's a good start! What do you think?"

What do I think, I ask myself. I breathe in deep and blow it out, trying to calm the swirly feeling in my gut. I look good. I look like not me. I like the face in the mirror, but then I imagine leaving the house like this, people looking at me, kids my age, teachers, and suddenly want to throw up. I hold my breath until the feeling goes away. I can't say all this to Moira. She's so determined to help me, even if it's not the kind of help I know what to do with.

"It looks good," I say. "It makes my face feel weird, though. Stiff. Can I wash it off now?"

"I guess so," says Moira. She looks disappointed. Maybe even a little hurt. "I bought some of this stuff for you, though, so you can practice on your own. You look so pretty this way!"

"Yeah," I say. "Pretty." If someone asked if I wanted to be

pretty I'd say yes, of course, who doesn't? But still, I hurry to the bathroom and wash it all off. It's harder to scrub off than I expected, and for a while my face looks like a horror movie mask, but eventually my skin is red and blotchy but clean. Lingering traces of excitement and unease don't rinse down the drain with the blush.

Next Moira makes me watch her put makeup on her own face, so I can see how it's done. A memory rises, sharp as glass, the two of us hanging out in Uncle Roderick's room as he painted his face. He worked as a drag queen when he lived in New York City, and often said he didn't want to lose those skills. We both loved watching him, like it was a TV show. I once asked if I could be a drag queen too. Moira explained that was only for boys but Uncle Roderick said I could grow up to be whatever I wanted. Moira would ask him for techniques, tips, and sometimes he would let her brush blush on his cheeks or spread foundation on his jaw. Maybe if I thought of myself as a drag queen I wouldn't have washed off that makeup so fast. But that's ridiculous.

It must be obvious that I'm not having fun, because Moira finally takes pity on me and changes the subject slightly.

"I'm thinking about joining the band! Flute, or clarinet. Or maybe the yearbook committee, so I can take pictures of everyone!"

"Sounds fun," I say, examining an eyelash curler. Who wants curly eyelashes?

"What about you? Maybe you could try out for the soft-ball team, or the track team."

"You know I hate sports."

"Okay, but have you ever tried? Maybe you'd like them! And besides, it's cool to be a girl who's good at sports. There are other options, though. Like, you could run for student government. Or yearbook with me! But seriously, you should pick *something*."

"Why?" I demand. "I've never been really into clubs and sports and things, what makes you think that's going to change just because we're at a new school?"

Moira's cleaning the makeup brushes with some sort of wipe. There's a pause; she's not looking at me but obviously thinking about what to say. "You don't have to change," she starts carefully, "but don't you want to? All of my other friends are girls I met through, you know, *doing* stuff. Finding people who are interested in the same kinds of things I am. And there are even more things to do in middle school! New people, new everything. Don't you want that? Something to do after school besides your homework?"

"I don't want anything else to change," I mutter. I'm already picking the Strawberrylicious off my fingernails.

She freezes, then looks up at me. I shouldn't have said that. I don't want to talk about it. But I had been looking forward to middle school too, excited to read new books and learn new things. Suddenly I'm imagining the halls lined with girls who look like movie stars, pointing and laughing.

To her credit, Moira looks like she genuinely feels bad. "I'm sorry, Bug. Your uncle just died and all. But I don't want us to feel left out once we start school. We've got to come up with a plan before it's too late." What she's not saying is that I'd be the one left out. Not her. And she might not stay out there with me.

Is she right? I don't know if she's right. "Can I think about it?" I ask. It all seems like too much. I guess she's trying to make sure I'm ready, but I don't think all this advice is really for me. She's more worried about future-her than now-me.

"Sure," she says, with a slightly forced smile. "You've got the whole rest of the summer, I guess." The weeks stretch out in front of me, slow and hot, the finish line shimmering like a mirage. I don't know who I'll be when I cross over.

five

I can't sleep. That face in the mirror fills the dark behind my eyelids. I know I'm a girl and all, but I've never thought of myself like *that*. Like a real girl, someone who looks the part. I'm always self-conscious of how hard I'm pretending, picking up cues from how other girls act but never quite getting it right. That girl looking back at me looked like she got it right.

Uncle Roderick always understood that about me. One time he brought some man over for dinner, a prospective boyfriend named Parker. Parker worked in fashion down in Boston and after dinner he started telling me about all the cute dresses he would make for me, sketching them out on a notepad. He said we might live in the country but I didn't have to dress like it. I doodled on the knee of my threadbare jeans with a ballpoint pen until he left, and Uncle Roderick never brought him around again. The next day he took me hiking in his most ragged outfit and we built a fort out of branches and vines, getting absolutely filthy in the process.

I hear a rustling that sounds like Moira sitting up in her

sleeping bag. She always has to pee in the middle of the night, so I don't think much of it until she starts screaming at the top of her lungs.

I jump out of my sleeping bag and almost out of my skin. "What is it? What's wrong?" The room is pitch-black.

"I don't know! It hurts! Help me!"

I fumble for the closest lamp. Light floods the room and I see Moira sitting on the floor, clutching her left foot, blood trickling between her fingers.

"What happened?" I rush over, skidding around a tiny pile of broken glass and sticky pink liquid that's matted onto the rug.

"I don't know," she says again, the shriek still in her voice. "I got up to go to the bathroom, and stepped in . . . oh my god, what is that? Is that my blood?" She starts sobbing, and I put my arms around her awkwardly until she has herself under control.

"It's definitely not blood," I say, poking at the strange heap of glass and color. The chemical scent makes it hard to breathe. "It's too pink to be blood. It looks like one of the nail polish bottles broke." It was the Strawberrylicious, but Moira doesn't need that information right now. "Let me look at your foot."

Moira doesn't usually mind blood, but she whimpers at the sight of me picking little shards of glass out of her skin. I can't figure out how to get the nail polish off the bottom of her foot, but I grab some Band-Aids from the bathroom and patch her up. I'm glad Mom sleeps like a stone. If she heard us, I know she'd come running, but she doesn't need to be woken up for this.

Moira calms down gradually. A question nudges the corner of my mind; I want to leave it alone but Moira brings it up.

"I don't get it," she says. "How did that bottle get over there? I thought I put it in the pile with everything else. And how the heck did it break by itself?"

"Maybe it rolled off the pile?" I suggest. I don't sound very convincing, but forge ahead. "And it probably broke when you stepped on it. Right?"

Moira shakes her head vehemently. "No, it was broken already. I would have felt it pop. I stepped right into that pile of broken glass." The tears rise in her voice again. "I thought you said there were no new ghosts."

"I did," I tell her, hoping she can't hear my uncertainty. But the old ghosts would never do something like this. They don't *do* things, period. "We'll figure it out in the morning."

"I want to go home," she sniffles.

"It's the middle of the night," I say. "Let's try to go back to sleep. You can go home once it's light out." She pulls her sleeping bag close to mine, and neither of us falls asleep easily, ears pricked for the sound of shattering glass or anything else.

* * *

I wake up to the smell of pancakes and bacon. Moira is still sound asleep, drooling a little, and I don't want to wake her. She had a rough night.

I pad into the kitchen, squinting a little against the morning sun. "G'morning," I say, yawning in the middle of "morning." Mom is bustling around, bacon stacked onto a platter next to her and pancake batter sizzling in our big old cast-iron pan.

"Good morning, sunshine, how was the sleepover? Is Mo—Moira—still sleeping?"

I fill Mom in on Moira's accident. Mom suggests that a mouse had knocked it off the pile, and that Moira actually had broken it when she stepped on it but didn't realize it because she was half-asleep. "But don't say that to Moira. She might start worrying about a mouse-transmitted disease."

"Probably. That makes sense," I say. And it does, kind of, but I don't think Moira is heavy enough to break a nail polish bottle just from stepping on it in bare feet. But Mom would just come up with another logical explanation. I open my mouth to tell her about the makeover Moira gave me, but can't get a word out. It's too much to talk about. I load up a plate and sit down at the table to eat.

Moira comes in a few minutes later, looking as groggy as I feel. Strong black tea would be good for both of us, but

I don't suggest it. She's walking gingerly, limping a little. "Mmm, pancakes. Thanks, Sabrina."

"Of course, Moira. Bug told me about your accident last night—how is your foot?"

"Okay, I guess. It was so scary, though. I don't know how it happened." Her voice trembles a little, but she manages to stay calm.

"It sounds scary! Why didn't you girls wake me up?"

We both shrug. I didn't want to keep Mom from a good night's sleep. She had spent so many overnights at Uncle Roderick's side. I wonder if she understands, because she drops it. "Well sweetie, I'm sure there's some logical explanation. It's not bleeding anymore, right?" Moira shakes her head. "Good. Have some pancakes."

She goes home not long after breakfast. I don't mind. I'm relieved that she didn't bring up our makeup experiments to my mom, and that my mom didn't ask why there had been a pile of mascara, blush, and nail polish on the living room floor in the first place. I try to clean the Strawberrylicious off the rug, scrubbing it with every cleaning solution I can find. And think about what could have moved it to the center of the carpet, what could have broken it. There's no single answer that makes sense.

The only way to get the nail polish off the rug is to trim away the tips of it with a pair of nail scissors. Mom comes in and I freeze, wondering if maybe I shouldn't be cutting something that won't grow back, but she doesn't comment. Just plops down next to me and asks what Moira and I got up to last night.

I keep my attention on the rug, making the tiniest snips possible. "She brought over some makeup. We were messing around with it. She says it's because middle school will be different."

Mom takes a deep breath, then lets it out gently. "Would you like me to buy you some makeup too?"

I shake my head. It's hard to get words out. We both know there's a huge collection of makeup in Uncle Roderick's bedroom that neither of us will touch. "No," I croak. "Thanks. Maybe later."

"Whenever you're ready, sweetheart." Her voice is only a little shaky. I can't imagine what ready will feel like. Mom leaves me to my task, and soon the patch of rug looks like it's gotten a bad haircut. I give up and go outside.

Uncle Roderick always complained that there was nowhere nearby to buy good makeup, anyway. Every time he went down to New York to visit his drag queen friends he would come back with a small suitcase full of fancy brands. Sometimes Mom would photograph him after he painted himself up.

His drag name had been Anita Life. I used to laugh hysterically over that, and come up with names for other, more ridiculous queens: Anita Bath, Ivanna Pee. Dumb kid things. When I got older, and understood more about what he had given up by moving here with Mom and newborn me, his drag name started to seem a little sad. I hope he didn't really feel that way. Now it's too late to know for sure.

Mom, on the other hand, has never worn makeup in her life. Or at least, not in the life I've known her in. All of her shirts and jeans are crusty with glue and paint and marker. I've seen old pictures of her, with my dad, where she's all dressed up with red lips and styled hair, but there's not a lot of opportunities to get fancy in the middle of nowhere. I wonder if she misses it, or if she's happier this way.

The closest village is about five miles away, with a grocery store, a post office, a library, and some other little shops. We're about an hour's drive from the nearest city, which is probably more of a large town.

The bus that took me to elementary school picked up some kids an hour before it got to my stop, which is a ten-minute drive from my house. And it still took another hour to get to school, picking up other kids along the way. We all barely have neighbors, let alone neighborhoods. I've never even been in a traffic jam.

A lot of kids at school complain about how isolated it is out here. They always talk about how much better it would be to live in a city, or even a more populated suburb, with malls and fast-food chains an easy bike ride away. A lot of houses, like mine, don't even have cable TV or a stable Internet connection. That's why my mom is on the creative side of the card business, and Ellen takes care of the business side. It's hard to communicate with clients when a passing cloud (or spirit) interrupts your Wi-Fi connection. Moira successfully begged her mom for a cell phone, but it doesn't even get a signal at my house. I might have begged for one despite that, if I had anyone to call.

But I love it out here. If we lived near a mall, or a beach town, or a Main Street, I'd spend my entire life wandering in and out of the same stores, never buying anything, never seeing anyone besides the same old people or interchangeable old tourists. I'd make friends or enemies or frenemies with local kids who were just as bored as I was. Maybe one kid would be the shoplifter, another would be the bully no one would confront. I'd be the kid that no one liked enough to invite out on purpose, but no one disliked enough to avoid. There would be no reason for me not to get along with anyone, but I'd always know, somehow, that the other kids were on the inside of every experience, and I was just watching.

Living here means I've never had any choice but to be by myself, though, which means I've never had to feel bad about it.

Of course, I was never completely alone. Uncle Roderick was always right there. Now that he's gone, maybe I'll find myself wishing for a mall. I hope not.

six

Since camp isn't happening this year, I'm spending whole days out of doors. Staring up at clouds, climbing trees, reading. Looking for minnows in the creek. Like a character in a book, some old-fashioned story about a wholesome childhood before the Internet existed. I mean, it barely exists at my house, but I still *know* about it, and sometimes Moira will show me memes or videos or whatever. Knowing about the Internet but not having it is very different from it not existing. I don't miss it, but I also have a sense that there's a lot that I am missing.

"The girl ran barefoot over the lawn, a warm breeze caressing her face," I imagine. That girl sounds like she's having fun.

"She brushed the dirt from her cutoff jean shorts. I sure could go for some lemonade, she thought, wiping sweat from her brow."

I want to be that girl. Not myself. Everything she does sounds significant. Real, somehow, in a way that my life isn't. When I do those things they're just . . . the things that

I'm doing. Not some plucky heroine, just a . . . just me. Even reading on the porch sounds more interesting when I pretend to be a character in a book doing it. Reading A Book On The Porch, instead of just reading a book on the porch.

I should be grateful that Uncle Roderick died toward the beginning of summer. If it was winter it would be too cold to play outside, with clear, sharp-toothed icicles ringing the eaves. Springtime would be wet, and still cold. And autumn is already creepy enough. But it's hard to feel grateful that the world is overflowing with green and life and heat, and none of it is for him.

The heavy door to Uncle Roderick's room is always shut tight. When I have to get to my bedroom I tiptoe past as quickly as possible, holding my breath till I'm safe in my room. Sometimes if I'm trying to fall asleep I see his door looming in my mind's eye, like it's about to spring open. I never imagine what's on the other side. I'm not ready to go there.

Empty rooms feel hollow. Uncle Roderick's room feels solid. Like someone is still in there, even when I know Mom is downstairs. A presence, not a person, waiting for the right moment to make itself known. "The girl knew there was nothing to be afraid of," claims the narrator in my head.

I keep thinking about the phrase "rest in peace," and hoping that it's true. It sounds better than just dead. Meanwhile, my uncle-less days take on a rhythm. Play outside all day, or read on the porch. A quiet dinner with Mom. Reading on the couch, curled up next to her as she watches TV. Shower, then brush my teeth while reading, to avoid any unsettling face-changes in the mirror. Hurry past Uncle Roderick's room, collapse into bed, fall asleep eventually, wake up, repeat.

A few days of quiet. And then the dreams start.

I'm sitting in a cold, dark room. But it's not a room. I know this because there are no walls, no ceiling, it goes on forever and I'm alone in the void. I'm sitting on a small, rickety chair at a table, a mirror propped up in front of me. The table is strewn with eyelash curlers, rusted shut. Nail polish bottles, empty, the crusted red like so much blood. Blush and eye shadow the color of mold, because they are mold. I'm holding a tube of lipstick in my hand, it's bright pink, the only necessary color in the world. I know what to do with this. I look into the cracked and dusty mirror that's on the table in front of me and start to put it on. I smear it onto my teeth, down my jaw, there's no way to be careful because skulls don't have lips and that's what's staring at me in the mirror, empty holes for eyes and an unhappy grin stained pink. A figure moves behind me in the mirror, I whip around to see who it is and

suddenly I'm awake, gasping for air, sprawled on my bed, sheet twisted around my legs, fan blowing softly across my body. I stare up at my ceiling, breathing hard. Morning sun pouring through the window. It was a dream, I tell myself. Just a bad dream. Uncle Roderick would say it represents something I'm afraid of. Skulls mean death, right? Of course I'm afraid of death. Especially now. I focus on slowing down my pounding heart, deep breaths to stop the shaking.

Slowly, slowly, the dream-fear slips away. And what was even so scary about it? Okay, the empty, dark space was awful. The skull-me was freaky. And the old moldy makeup. But nothing *bad* happened, not really.

Usually my dreams are single moments, weird flashes that I barely remember in the morning, but this felt like I was really sitting at the table. And now that I'm awake, I remember feeling like there was someone in there with me. I have to get my mind off this, so I swing my legs over the side of my bed, sit up, and choke back a scream.

My room is a *mess*. The drawers have been pulled completely out of their sockets, the contents strewn all over the floor. The doors to my closet yawn open, my clothes pulled off the hangers and flung around the room. My bedside lamp, lying on its side. The upended bookshelf.

My brain turns over every possible explanation. Burglars looking for something? But there's nothing that would be in my room. And I would have heard them do this. Did I do this, in my sleep? A ghost? But ghosts don't do this kind of thing. At least, they never have before.

Every explanation seems equally likely, and equally unlikely. I don't know which one I want to believe.

I stare at everything wrong in my room, and my breathing gets quicker and quicker until I'm panting, then sobbing, my shoulders quake and my palms press against my face slippery with tears and snot and that narrator that's always murmuring in my head suggests that this is the part of the story where I cry over my uncle's death and maybe start to heal but I don't think that's what's happening but I don't know what's happening and I can barely breathe but I'm being as quiet as I can so Mom doesn't hear. The time on my alarm clock, still plugged in but on the floor, is 8:14 a.m., which means I have sixteen minutes to pull myself together and clean before Mom gets up, because I can't explain this to her.

So I do. I stop crying. Wipe my face. It's easy to dump things in their drawers. Shove things into the closet. Books back on the shelf, I can organize them later. I clean up enough so that when Mom knocks gently on my door, asks what I want for breakfast, I can open it up and she doesn't see anything wrong. She's got enough to worry about right now.

Moira invited me over today. Her dad built their house, like, fifteen years ago, close to the tiny center of our tiny town. It's too new for ghosts, and I'm suddenly so grateful for that.

Maybe we'll watch a movie, or play a board game. Makeovers are more like sleepover games, right? She wouldn't want to do that two hangouts in a row. I climb on my bike and head over. This ride is so familiar to me, I sometimes envision a rut, exactly the shape of my wheels, leading between our houses. Like if I closed my eyes and just pedaled I'd be guided safely there. Sometimes Uncle Roderick would ride over with me, "Just to get my blood pumping," he'd say, and we'd yell terrible knock-knock jokes or alert each other to chipmunks or interesting birds. But I've ridden back and forth by myself so many times. There's no reason to sense his presence at my side, or notice it missing.

Memories of the dream, that endless dark room, keep flashing across my eyes. I've never had a dream like that before, one that I can remember like a story hours later. And the disaster in my bedroom. They must be related, it can't be a coincidence. Something is going on, I think, something new. There's a steep uphill stretch, usually I walk my bike up it, but today I pedal as fast as possible so all I can focus on are the burning muscles in my legs, my lungs fighting for air. I never bother knocking once I get to their house, just pull open the door and call out a hello to Moira's mom, Ellen.

"Hi, Bug," she calls back. "Everyone's down in the basement."

Everyone? I wasn't expecting an everyone. I pull open

the door to the basement and hear it ringing with laughing voices. I stay on the top step for a moment. Moira doesn't know I've come yet, she won't know if I leave. I can make up some excuse to her mom. I don't like this kind of surprise, having to be around a whole group when I was only expecting one person. But I don't want to go back to my house, and whatever might be waiting for me there. And someone must have noticed the open door, because the voices quiet, and I hear Moira call "Bug? Is that you?"

I clench my fists tight, force on a smile, and head downstairs. Moira's basement is like a second living room, fully furnished with couches and a bathroom and a huge TV, nothing like our dank cellar. There are five girls on the fluffy rug, huddled in a circle. I recognize them all, besides Moira, obviously. Emily and Madeleine were in the other sixth-grade class. Isla and Olive were in mine. We weren't friends, but I'm not really friends with anyone except Moira, so that doesn't mean anything. They've always been nice enough. Maybe this will be okay.

They're surrounding a big book full of thumbnail photographs. A yearbook?

"Hey Bug!" says Moira. "We're looking at a Maplewood Middle School yearbook. Isla's sister is an eighth grader there, so she brought hers over from last year."

"We're trying to figure out which boys are cuter in their pictures than in real life," says Madeleine.

"And vice versa!" Olive chimes in. Everyone giggles. I

force a giggle-like sound out of my throat, but it's a beat too late and sounds more like a strangled wheeze. I quickly move to crouch between Moira and Emily, sure that I can play this game. I think boys are cute, right? Boys are cute.

I fake my way through the conversation. I point and giggle, pretending to be disappointed when Isla says that this one boy with a nice smile always licks his hands and then tries to touch you. Sometimes my mind drifts back to that cluttered table in the cold, the cracked mirror, what's waiting for me in my bedroom, but I snap myself back as quickly as I can, agreeing with whatever the other girls are saying.

Ever since Moira started talking about cute boys, and which ones she wanted to kiss, I haven't known what to say. I can observe that some boys are nice to look at, but I don't know what to do with that. I definitely don't want to smush my face against theirs, or have their grimy hands hold mine.

I said that to Uncle Roderick once, and he asked if I felt different about girls. I thought about it, since I knew there wasn't anything wrong with girls liking girls. But I didn't want to smush my face against theirs, either. Maybe it's something I'll figure out when I'm older. But if I admit my indifference everyone will think I'm weird. Weirder.

Finally Isla puts the yearbook in her backpack, and we troop upstairs to make lunch. We're eating peanut butter sandwiches on the porch (me trying not to think about what a skull would look like with peanut butter in its mouth) when Madeleine suddenly asks, "What kind of a name is Bug, anyway? I know that's what everyone calls you, but it can't be your real name, right?"

Words freeze in my throat for a second, and I swallow hard. "It's not her real name," Moira pipes up. "It's just a nickname. Her—"

"My uncle gave it to me," I blurt out, before Moira can say what my real name is. "He died a few weeks ago. He thought that my first steps were to get to him, but I was actually chasing after a ladybug that got trapped in the living room. He started calling me Bug, and it stuck. I like it. Even my mom says it's better than the name she gave me. Because I'm, like, small, I guess? I dunno." I'm babbling. I don't usually blurt out random things like this, but I desperately want Moira not to tell them what my name is. And I don't want to tell them that I don't want them to know. It's too complicated all of a sudden. Like another part of my uncle will be gone, and like he'd know, and be disappointed. It's an unfamiliar kind of panic bubbling up through the peanut butter in my belly, and I guess Moira understands that something is going on, because she changes the subject.

"My mom says that a new family has moved into the old Baumler farmhouse, have you guys seen them?"

"That creepy old place?" Olive shudders. "I won't even

walk past that place after dark. Mega-haunted." Olive has never come over to my house. Not that I've ever invited her.

"Do you know who's living there?" asks Madeleine. "Maybe girls our age?"

"Or boys!" adds Emily.

"I'm not sure," says Moira. "If Mom finds out I'll text you all. And Bug, I'll . . . I'll let you know when we hang out."

I'm pretty sure that now they're all wondering what kind of freak doesn't text. But after a minute Isla changes the subject to all the different stores she would put into a mall if there was one nearby.

"Hot Topic, for sure, at least for funny buttons and stuff."

"H and M!" Emily sighs longingly.

They keep talking about stores that aren't the Target that Mom drives me to if I need more socks, and the rest of the day is like I'm sitting in that endless cave from my dream, watching myself through the dark mirror like it's a TV screen. Like it's a show where a happy group of girls are talking about normal middle school things like clothes and makeup, and one kid keeps trying to join the conversation but doesn't know how.

I don't think clothes and makeup are dumb. They're not the most interesting topic of conversation for me, but I don't think they're silly or anything. They're just far away from me. A few months ago Moira got a subscription to some teen magazine, and gave me her old issues once she was done with them. I figured that those magazines taught girls how to be girls. Like that was how they all learned this stuff, and after reading them I would know too. But apparently that's not how teen magazines work. You're supposed to understand it already, somehow.

I hear my name and snap back to the conversations. "What?" I ask, interrupting Moira as she started a sentence with "Our moms—"

"Oh, I was just asking how you two became friends," says Madeleine. Is it just my imagination, or is there a question inside that question? Like why Moira would be friends with someone like me?

Moira tucks a strand of hair behind her ear. "Our moms started a business together," she says, glancing over at me and then away. "We've basically been friends since we were babies."

"Well, we were enemies first," I blurt out. Why did I say that? But there's no choice but to keep going. "We didn't get along for years, and we fought about *everything*, but since we were forced to play together we eventually figured it out. And now we're friends! Right?" (Stop talking, Bug, you're not helping anything.)

"I had a friend like that," says Emily. "We have the same birthday, so our parents became friends in the hospital. We had all our birthday parties together until kindergarten, until we started wrestling in the ice-cream cake and our parents realized we hated each other."

"Well, we don't hate each other now!" Moira says cheerily.

She smiles at me, and I smile back, but both our eyes cut away quickly.

Moira's mom stops by the living room to say that my mom called, she's been running errands and will pick me up in about an hour. By the time she pulls up, the summer sun is starting to dip behind the trees and my face hurts from the interested expression it's been frozen into for hours.

Emily and Madeleine just left, so I say goodbye to Isla, Moira, and Olive. "Bye, Bug!" says Isla. "I had so much fun today, let's definitely sit at the same lunch table once school starts."

"Ooh, yeah!" says Olive. "I had a good time too. We're going out of town until school starts, but see you in September!"

It sounds like they mean it, and I'm suddenly warm all over. Maybe they don't think I'm weird? Maybe I did a good job of pretending. The fake smile on my face expands into a real one. "Bye!" I say. "Moira, thanks for inviting me! TTYL!" I'm not sure if "TTYL" is something people say in real life, or only in books about the Internet, but they all laugh and wave as I run down to the car.

"How was it?" Mom asks as I slam the door, my bike stashed in the back. Crumpled tissues spill out of the cup holder.

"Fun?" I say. Ask, maybe, since Mom hears the question

in my voice and looks at me with a question mirrored in her eyes.

I rest my head against the car window. It's warm. "There were some other girls there too, Isla and Madeleine and them, and . . . I don't know. Moira and I have never been the same, you know? Usually when it's just her and me it doesn't matter. But when it's her and me and other people, it's always been obvious. That she's more like them, and I'm not."

Mom nods, but slowly. "I know that you and Moira have always been two very different kinds of kids. But you've turned into good friends these last few years, right? Has something else changed lately?"

"I think so? It's not like we're getting into fights. I still like her. And she seems to still like me. But I got so bored today! We didn't do anything except talk about, like, boys and shopping and stuff. Is that the only thing anyone's going to want to talk about for the next two years?" It's more than that, really. They seem to fit together like puzzle pieces, and I'm a shape cut out of cardboard. It looks right if you squint, but it can't snap into place.

Mom is quiet for a minute. I wonder if she's going to ask why I don't like talking about those things. I don't have a reason. But instead she says, "Well, you'll be meeting a lot of new kids soon. Maybe you'll find some who are more like you."

"Yeah," I say. But I don't know what "more like me" means. I imagine chattering knots of kids in a cafeteria, some talking about sports, some playing games, some doing each other's hair and others talking about music or movies or books or video games, cracking jokes or fighting or telling secrets. And I imagine myself floating past all of them, always on the outside, no one noticing me, because there's nothing to notice. Like their groups form a complex molecule, a perfect organism, impenetrable and complete and I'm a speck of dust caught in the light, visible and alone and insignificant. But I can't describe that to Mom. And I don't want to. So I just say, "Maybe I'll have more friends than just Moira soon."

Mom says she hopes so. I wonder if she hopes that for herself too. We'll both need other people to spend time with, now that it's just the two of us. After all, she's as alone as I am.

seven

My insides start to squirm as we pull up in front of the house, eaves peering down at me like hooded eyes. I keep my eyes averted from the dark window on the second floor that Uncle Roderick used to wave to me from. He won't be there. He's at peace. If I see something behind the glass, it won't be him. I suppress a shiver as we walk in through the tall front door, a chill gusting from somewhere in the house through my body to dissipate in the heat of an early July night.

The afternoon at Moira's house hadn't been the best time, but it was better than wandering around my house endlessly replaying the dream from last night, afraid of whatever destroyed my room—my own sleeping self, or something else.

I'm on edge all night, but nothing unusual happens. Mom makes dinner, hot dogs and fresh corn. I make the salad. Some cold breezes, some creaking, just the normal spirits moving around. Nothing paying attention to me.

While we eat she tells me about the different designs

she's coming up with for condolence cards. "The dumb things people have been telling me about your uncle have been helping," she says, the smile on her face only slightly forced. "Like, one of our cousins pulled out the old 'he's in a better place right now' nonsense. As if somewhere could be better than having dinner with you, right now. So I'm playing around with a card that has someone in a five-star spa, surrounded by Jacuzzis and servants carrying fancy snacks, with a guy remembering his cramped little house with a screaming baby saying 'I thought they said I was going to a better place.' Something like that. Get it?"

"I like it," I tell her. "Do you think people will buy it? It's not too depressing?"

"Hey, if people buy the fill-in-the-blanks, they'll buy this."

"Probably," I say. The fill-in-the-blank cards are the simplest ones Mom has ever made, and the best sellers. They're plain white, and the cover says "I'm Sorry That Your _____ Died." The inside type reads "It Really Sucks." There are a whole bunch of them on the mantel now, the blanks filled in with "Brother," "Uncle," or "Roderick." Some people might say they're insensitive, but they work. It sucks when someone dies. There's not much else to say.

"I guess that's one silver lining to come out of all this," I say, trying to sound cheerful and well-adjusted.

Mom cocks her head. "What do you mean?"

I don't know what I mean. That's just something people

say, whenever a situation could possibly be worse, and every situation could get worse, somehow. But now I have to defend my point.

"Well . . . you haven't designed any new cards in a while. And you've said that you don't like being a one-woman assembly line. It must be nice to work on a new project. Like a creative outlet."

That makes sense, even if it's dead wrong. And I need Mom to tell me that of course that's not true, that it will always be terrible that he left us, that a million new best-selling card ideas inspired by his loss can't make up for a single one of his terrible puns. When he was alive he would sometimes try to help Mom brainstorm, but he was too earnest, too sincere for her brand of dark humor.

But she nods and something shrivels up inside me. Maybe she thinks I'm doing okay. And that's what I want her to think. Isn't it? "Maybe you're right," she says. "I haven't wanted to tell you about this, but revenue has been down for a while. We're still hanging on, and Ellen is exploring other web-based options, but maybe some of the new cards I've been coming up with will do the trick."

I fidget with my napkin, avoid Mom's eyes, avoid glancing up at the mirror behind her head. I'm glad my mom has always treated me like an equal member of the household. I wish that being an equal member meant I could do more to help. "I'm done eating," I say, without responding to what she said. "Want me to clean up?"

She hugs me tight and then goes back to her studio. I do the dishes, staring fixedly into the sink the whole time. The kitchen used to be the heart of our home, but now it's just the room I'm in, by myself.

I'm not ready to go to my bedroom yet, so after dishes I look through the magazines that Moira's left at my house the past few months. I study the makeup tutorials like they are the Rosetta stone and try to figure out what's going on in the tampon ads. My period hasn't started yet, but it'll happen eventually. Maybe that's what I need, to actually start puberty, maybe then I'll feel like a girl.

I try to imagine myself growing up like that, filling out a bra, caring about what my hair looks like. I can't really imagine it. Trying to picture myself as a teenage girl is like staring at the sun, too bright to see, and it hurts. Thinking about being an adult, a woman, makes me feel like I'm looking up at the stars but there's nothing holding me to the earth, and I might fly off into the void at any moment. A squirmy, itchy sensation starts to expand in my stomach. I know your stomach can't itch from the inside, but that's what it's like.

I should put my room back in order. I'm more like Uncle Roderick than my mother in that way. Her studio is chaos, art supplies and papers everywhere. She knows where everything is, but there's no system that makes sense to anyone else.

Uncle Roderick was much more organized, and so am I. He and I used to spend hours arranging his clothes and makeup and jewelry, by color or brand or glitteriness. My bookshelf is always in alphabetical order by title, or author, or arranged by genre. This morning I just shoved everything generally in the right spot, so nothing is quite where it belongs.

I climb the stairs, listening for their normal creaks, and scurry past Uncle Roderick's room. The door is shut tight, with no one behind it listening to me dart past; any other feeling is just my imagination, just wishful thinking.

It takes an hour to get my room back to normal. Neatly folded clothes, paired socks. Books organized by color this time. The orderly, steady work slows down my racing mind, and I start to get that comfortable floatiness that Moira says is called ASMR, like a buzzing behind my eyes and a sense of stillness and quiet in my limbs. I imagine that I'm a well-behaved orphan, proving to potential adoptive parents what a perfect child I'll be if they just welcome me into their home, but this orphanage is filled with jealous, cruel girls who are trying to sabotage me at every turn because they want to be adopted first. I know I'm too old for make-believe, but no one has to know. I could play these quiet games for the rest of my life, be always in a story and never really here.

Eventually everything is back in perfect order, and my

eyelids are heavy. I don't want to fall asleep, but know I can't stay awake forever. Whatever happened last night probably won't happen again. And if it does, there's got to be some logical explanation. Even if the logical explanation is a ghost. I'll figure it out. I switch off my lamp, pull up my sheet, and eventually, somehow, drift off.

I'm in a mall, but can't walk. Every step is hard. Like being underwater, or buried waist-deep in sand. Like I'm so tired, I can't move my legs, but I have to. I'm in a store, an empty store, bare hangers and empty shelves. It's crowded with mannequins. They're all naked. Where are their clothes? Their bodies are smooth and featureless, like Barbie dolls. Blank faces. I try to move away from them but walking is almost impossible. Then they're not mannequins, they're Moira and Olive and Madeleine and Isla and Emily, and they're naked and looking down at me and I'm looking down at me wrapping my arms around myself. They start to laugh, not laughing at me, just laughing like friends laugh with each other, I try to join in but it sounds like wheezing, like screaming, like gasping for air, and they look at me with pity, standing tall and strong and straight while I'm hunched over myself arms wrapped around my chest and I try one more time to get away and

don't fall out of bed, but almost. I'm thrashing around, sweaty, out of breath again.

Another dream, like a story, like a message. My eyes are still shut, and I'm afraid to open them. Afraid to see if my room has been destroyed again. I tell myself that it's okay, over and over again, that I'll figure it out, and slowly, cautiously, work up the nerve to crack open my eyelids and look around.

My room is fine. Just the way I left it, closet door closed, books on their shelves, drawers shut tight. I smile, and stretch my way out of bed.

My feet hit the carpet. Well, one foot does. The other lands on something crisp that rustles under my foot. A note? I pick it up; it's a torn scrap of slightly yellowish paper, covered in writing. Or what looks like writing, at first glance. It could be my mom's handwriting, but hers also looks just like Uncle Roderick's. And on second glance, it doesn't really look like handwriting at all.

There aren't any words I can make out. It's covered in chicken-scratch symbols, looking enough like normal writing that my eyes refuse to accept that there's no message to read. I try turning it upside down, holding it up to the light, looking at each symbol individually and also letting my eyes relax, like there's some trick that will let me decipher it.

Aside from the strange writing, there's nothing else weird about it. It could be torn out from a notebook, or from the junk drawer in Mom's office. The writing isn't in blood or smudged calligraphy ink; it looks like a normal ballpoint pen. If I could just figure out what it said, it would look like a normal note from Mom. Maybe she left for the morning, went to the grocery store or is meeting with Moira's mom.

There's a knock at my door, and I jump. Mom asks if I'm up, says she's made breakfast. So there goes that theory. I tell her I just got out of bed, and will be down in a minute.

I'll ask Mom about this at breakfast. That's a good idea. I didn't want to tell her about my messed-up room, but there might be a good explanation for this note. Maybe she's learning about codes and wanted me to decipher it. Maybe she was just doodling, and it fell out of her pocket when she came in to kiss me good night. If I act like it's no big deal, she won't think I'm worried about anything. It might not be related to my bad dreams, or my suddenly more haunted house, at all.

There's a plate of scrambled eggs waiting for me at the kitchen table, and Mom's buttering toast as I sit down. She asks how I slept, I tell her, and then I place the note on the table. "Do you know what this is?" I ask, keeping my voice as nonchalant as possible. "It looks like your handwriting"— and Uncle Roderick's, I think—"but I can't figure out what it says."

She comes around and picks it up. Her brow furrows like mine must have, trying to make the unfamiliar strokes resolve into something she can read. She even turns it upside down, like I did, before giving up.

"Nope, I didn't write this. Where did you find it?"

My stomach twists. "Just around the house," I say, trying not to snatch it back too quickly. I crumple it up and stick it in my pocket. "It's probably just . . . it just showed up. Whatever." She looks at me, a little confused, like *What is up with my kid?* There's a quirk to her mouth like she's waiting for me to tell her what's going on, and I just can't.

She's never flat-out told me not to believe in ghosts, but always rolled her eyes when Uncle Roderick and I talked about the spirits we sensed drifting around. "It's just a house," she'd always say. "It's old, and creaky, and drafty, and the only spirits in it are ours." She never told us *not* to talk about that stuff, but she made Uncle Roderick serve on nightmare duty—vague terrors about ghosts and monsters that would start to fade away soon after waking up, not like my last few dreams, complex and crystal-clear. I learned early on not to talk to her about the mirrors, or the ghostly hands that grabbed at my hair or clothes. I never wanted her to think I was crazy. And the older I got, the more I wondered whether Uncle Roderick really believed, or if he just enjoyed telling stories.

Mom's answered one question, at least. This note is for me. Some presence is trying to send me a message, and messing up my room was just its first attempt. It's trying to communicate with me, and I have to figure out why. And what—or who—it is. This isn't something Mom and I will be able to figure out together.

"Can we get some chickens?" I blurt out. I don't know

where that came from. I'm eating eggs, and wanted to distract her, and that's all I could think of. But it's a good idea. I have a sudden vision of me gathering eggs, cradling them in an apron like a farm girl from some book about the olden days. "They're cute and soft, and we could have fresh-laid eggs, and use their poop for fertilizer. They'd make way better pets than a dog or a cat!" We had never had pets because Uncle Roderick was allergic. I guess we could get one now, but that would seem like another silver lining.

Mom turns back to the kitchen counter and cracks some more eggs for herself. "It's an interesting thought," she says. "But let's wait for business to pick up a bit more first, okay? Coops are expensive, so I'd rather hold off for now. But you could always do some research, on breeds and chicken care. It's not a bad idea."

I don't really want chickens. But I also don't not-want chickens, so maybe I'll look into them. Her mind is off the note now, which was my goal, and I finish my breakfast. Mom reads the newspaper while I attempt to read the comics, and the indecipherable note is a crisp ball, insistent against my thigh. I leave it there, a riddle.

eight

"No new ghosts," I had promised Moira, but what did I really know about the old ones? It's not like I had ever taken attendance, or found a notebook with names and death dates organized chronologically. There are some constants, like the cold spot in the living room, and the moods our rooms hold on to; the seriousness of Mom's bedroom, the friendliness of mine.

Sometimes Uncle Roderick and I would tell each other stories about the ghosts in our house. Very respectfully, of course—when I was little most of my stories would involve dying from an epic fart attack, or drowning in a bubble bath. But I remember Uncle Roderick sitting cross-legged in the living room one quiet winter evening, a battered cardboard box from the attic in front of him, pulling out old papers and albums and note cards that he said were records from past owners.

I was never that interested in the history of the house, except for the week he read aloud an old Baby-Sitter's Club book, the one where Dawn finds a secret passage in her house. I spent days knocking on every wall, pushing on nails, and trying to pry open fireplaces. If any house had a secret passageway or mysterious staircase or hidden room, it would be ours.

Of course I never found anything. And of course once I got tired of hunting I stopped wondering about who else wandered through these halls, paced up and down these stairs.

I was younger then. Now I'm older, with new questions, and I wonder if that box my uncle found will have answers.

It would make sense for our attic to be a creepy place, but it's actually pretty cozy. It's dark, sure, but also warmly lit by rays of sunshine that slant in through the tiny windows at the peak of the eaves. It smells like wood and leaves and age, and the floorboards creak in a friendly way. Specks of dust dance in the air, bathing the shaky stacks of boxes and old furniture in what could be glitter if you squint.

I'm looking for that box I remember Uncle Roderick digging through. Maybe every old house is this beset by spirits, but I want to learn something more particular about *this* house, *these* spirits. Who used to live here, who might still be lingering. Why they're still here, what they might want from me. If any of the hands that wrote in an old album or family tree, then left them for us to find, are also responsible for the message on my floor.

I've just started looking through boxes of my baby

clothes (The tiniest shoes! Were my feet ever that small?) and old report cards, trying to find something that looks like house documents, when I hear my name.

"Bug? *Bug!* Are you up there?" It's Moira, hollering up through the half-size door that leads to the attic.

I squinch my eyes shut for a second, frustrated. We *just* saw each other. But there's no other choice. "Yeah!" I call back, and hear her sigh heavily before thumping up the stairs.

"What are you doing up here?" she demands. "I looked everywhere for you except the basement, I refuse to go into your basement, but the attic is almost as bad!"

"I'm . . . looking for something," I tell her. "Were we supposed to hang out today?" I don't think so, but that's a more polite question than "What are you doing here" or "Why did you come over."

"Nope," she says, coughing dramatically, brushing dust off her pale green sundress. It looks nice against her complexion and red hair, and I'm suddenly very proud of myself for noticing something like that. Maybe the magazines are working after all. "Our moms are talking about business. And my mom made you guys a casserole. I had nothing else to do today, so I thought I'd tag along, is that okay?"

"Sure," I say, but I don't exactly mean it. We just spent a whole afternoon together, and I don't think I can handle more middle school or makeup conversations right now. If we're going to start drifting apart once school starts, we might as well practice giving each other space now.

"So? What are you doing up here?" she asks again, and my brain scrambles for an answer. I could tell her the truth: A mysterious note in strange handwriting appeared in my bedroom, it could be a message from beyond the grave, and I'm hoping that learning more about the history of the house and the ghosts that live here will help me figure out what's going on.

She'd go back downstairs, leaving me alone, which would be good. But then our moms would ask why we're not hanging out, and she'd tell them, which would be bad. I could tell her not to tell them, but then I'd have to come up with some other cover story for her to use, and I've already been running through these possibilities in my head for so long that she's staring at me and starting to look confused and worried.

"Just . . . I haven't been up here in a while," I say. "It's . . . fun to look through old stuff. Like my mom's old yearbooks. That sort of thing. I've been bored." It sounds like something I would do, at least.

Moira raises her eyebrows like she doesn't believe me, but I can practically see her admonish herself to be nice, since I'm the one with the dead uncle and all. It makes sense to be a little nostalgic. Probably.

"Okay," she says. "Mind if I look at stuff with you?"

"No," I say, trying not to sound too reluctant. We start digging through boxes together.

I give her one with my old baby clothes; I figure she can look through that for a long time. I'm not wrong. She's soon cooing and squealing over my old onesies and frilly dresses, while I look for that old, unlabeled box I remember Uncle Roderick carefully sorting through.

This tension is familiar from those years we didn't get along. Like one time, I told her that tomatoes were technically fruits, not vegetables. I've always loved fun little facts like that. She insisted that they were vegetables and I tried to explain, in my first-grade-scientist way, that fruit described a part of a plant, and vegetable was just a made-up category, but she yelled, far too confidently, "Then why do you have them in your *vegetable* garden?" It was such a dumb argument that I shoved her, hard, and she fell down. In my mind it was entirely justified, but she ran crying to our moms and I got sent to my room.

We were always arguing about little things like that. She'd elbow me if I beat her in a video game, I'd steal pretzels from her snack. No amount of reasoned, patient conversations with our parents made it better; we just endlessly got on each other's nerves. Then one year, when we were nine, she and her family went away for a month, and when they got back something had changed between us. We both grew up a little bit, just enough, to start cautiously exploring what we had in common: long bike rides, working in the vegetable (and fruit) garden, helping Uncle Roderick bake.

But now I wonder if we're going back to where we started. Or going somewhere new, but not together.

The search takes a while. I don't sense any spirits up here, but we're surrounded by other kinds of ghosts, old furniture and broken kitchen utensils and keepsakes that must have belonged to my grandparents or great-grandparents. I'm only half listening to Moira, who's moved on to old yearbooks and is exclaiming about how tiny we all were. And then I find the box.

I sit down with a thump and gingerly remove the lid. It's full of yellowed papers, carbon copies, some in old-fashioned type and others in spidery handwriting.

Moira notices my sudden excitement. "What's all that?" she asks, standing up on her knees to see better.

"House stuff," I manage to croak out, careful not to sound too invested. "It's interesting, actually. Information about the people who used to live here."

"Huh," says Moira. She puts our preschool yearbook back into the box and comes over. I carefully pull out folders and loose papers, and she helps me spread them out on the floor. I'm surprised this has caught her interest, but at least I don't have to explain why it's caught mine. There's a warmth between us now, and my earlier grumpiness is suddenly, unexpectedly washed away by how glad I am to have a friend here with me.

I already know my great-grandparents got this place before Mom and Uncle Roderick were born. We find an old deed that says they bought it way back in the 1960s from the Paterson family. And unless they bought it from another family with the same last name, the Patersons originally built it in 1843 and lived in it for over a century.

We learn a little bit, not as much as I had hoped for. According to an old blueprint, my bedroom has always been a children's bedroom. Mom's office, which has always felt cold and formal to me, had once been a servant's bedroom. Uncle Roderick's room, with its massive closet, is labeled "Dressing Room" in another set of blueprints, and apparently our living room wasn't added onto the house until 1868. I had been hoping for something like death certificates, or an extremely detailed family tree, that might have information on who died here in the hundred-plus years the Patersons filled up the place, but no such luck. And none of the writing on the old papers matches the writing in the note I found, not even close.

Moira stretches and yawns. "Well, that was an interesting trip through Vermont history. I wish my house was old and cool like this one." Her dad, an architect, designed their place. It looks like a futuristic gingerbread house, basically a log cabin with acute angles and too much glass.

"At least you know there aren't any ghosts in yours," I say.

"Good point. Any new ones?"

I hesitate. How much can I say, without making her worry? "You know . . . it's not like I've ever counted. Maybe this place is like the Grand Central Station of the spirit world, always new ones coming and going. Or maybe it's just one very grumpy Paterson that's stuck around this whole time."

Moira, sitting cross-legged on the floor, leans in closer to me. "Do you remember when I saw the ghost in the hallway?" she asks quietly.

I do. We were eight years old, coming up to my bedroom from the kitchen with an armload of snacks. I was behind her and didn't see anything, but Moira froze, dropped the bowl of Goldfish crackers she'd been cradling, and screamed bloody murder. She says she saw a little girl darting into Uncle Roderick's room, wearing an old-fashioned dress, something jerky and not right about her. But we had just finished watching a movie about an evil doll. And I had gotten used to the presences floating around my house, and never once saw something that resembled a human being, so I always thought it was just her imagination. Or she was trying to play a trick on me. But that's why our sleepovers are usually at her house, and why she doesn't like to come upstairs.

"Of course," I say. "But I've never seen anything like that."

"Maybe it was Zelda Paterson," she says. That was a name we came across, some girl who lived here in the early 1900s.

I force out a laugh, and it's strangely loud in this

high-ceilinged space. If this were a horror movie, we would have found an old diary that mysteriously ends at a blood-splattered page, or a bunch of newspaper articles about a mass murder or mysterious disappearance. Dusty old records of past residents didn't tell us anything conclusive.

"It could have been," I agree, because, who knows. "Come on, let's go downstairs. I'm hungry." I'm not really hungry, but for some reason I feel like we shouldn't speak their names so casually. I don't want to attract their attention.

Moira and her mom leave before dinner, so it's another quiet meal at the end of our long table. Buttered rice, broccoli, baked chicken. Plain, not bad, but I can't help imagining what this would look like if Uncle Roderick had cooked it. Wild rice, or purple cauliflower, or blackened chicken. Something with pizzazz. This is okay, though. "What did you girls get up to today?" Mom asks.

There are generations of Patersons swirling around us, but whatever is trying to get my attention, I don't think it's one of them. I can't imagine that they want anything from me, especially not all of a sudden. But something is, something does, my shoulders are around my ears, hunched up anxiously. I force myself to stretch, to relax. "We were in the attic," I reply. "Looking at my old baby clothes and your yearbooks and things." I take a bite of rice. It's buttery and salty, and suddenly I'm grateful for the comfort of something simple.

"Just a jaunty stroll down memory lane?" Mom asks.

There's an undercurrent of curiosity in her voice, like she knows there's something else going on.

"Yup," I say, as casually as I can. "We found your senior year class picture. Why was your hair so awful?"

She laughs. "It was the nineties, my modern child. Everyone thought we looked good. Your uncle did my makeup for me."

A chill gust of air whispers past me. I look to see if my mom notices it, if she shivers, but she doesn't react.

"How was your meeting?" I ask, peeling away a strip of chicken.

She shrugs. "It was . . . okay. We're exploring some new avenues, new possibilities. Trying to make enough to send you to camp next year!"

Her tone is chipper, but she's looking down at her plate, not at me. Like there's something she's hiding. But Mom would never keep anything important from me. Maybe she and Moira's mom had an argument, I know grown-ups argue about business sometimes. Or maybe she still feels bad that I couldn't go to camp.

"It's okay," I say. "It's been nice to hang out around here all summer." That's not true, exactly, but it would have been weird at camp this year. I'd either have to tell everyone what had happened, or not tell anyone what had happened. Both options would be hard. At least here, there's no one to tell or not tell.

I go to bed at my normal time but lie awake for hours, trying to read. Uncle Roderick would sometimes puzzle over his dreams at the breakfast table, trying to figure out what they meant. Mom said that they didn't mean anything, they were just his brain sorting through the mental junk drawer left behind from the day. My dreams always felt like that, random and meaningless and easily forgotten, so I was inclined to agree with her. Now, I don't want to go to sleep, don't want to hear what my mind—or something else—is trying to tell me. But of course I can't stay awake forever, and as I start to drift off I think, "What now?"

I'm in a store, a dressing room surrounded by dresses, frilly dresses, polka-dotted or striped or flowery or bright, puffy sleeves, poofy skirts, all of them are made for babies and toddlers and little girls, but they've been left here for me, I have to wear them or something bad will happen. My hands reach out and pick up the first one, white with pink roses sewn all over it, I am so huge and it is so small, but my head squeezes through the neck hole, my arms shove through the sleeves, it's so tight around my waist, it cuts. I look in the mirror and my body is exploding around it, red marks bright where skin rubs against fabric, but I don't have a choice. I grab the next dress, a frothy yellow, and it's worse. The cloth whines as my head pushes through the top, the sound of seams giving way as I tug it down over my torso, cracking my rib cage around my thudding heart and struggling lungs. And a third, white and lacy, it doesn't rip and neither does the next dress, each one hurts more and I can't stop putting them on and they are so hot and so tiny and my body is getting bigger and bigger and nothing works, they itch worse than poison ivy, I want to take the dresses off and my skin along with them. I can't breathe, my heart is pounding like a drum, I keep trying over and over until they fit right until they fit like they're supposed to until I look like I'm supposed to and the curtain keeping me hidden is ripped aside and I whip around and

somehow my top sheet has wound itself around my body like a rope, it's tight across my chest. I'm awake, and I'm okay. I can breathe. I hear my heart pattering away in my ears, but as I take some deep breaths it slows, quiets. I unwind the sheet, it's morning, and my room looks fine. No notes on the floor from beyond the grave. Nothing trying to get my attention. Maybe this one was just a junk-drawer dream. Even if it felt like someone was about to come into the dressing room with me. Like someone was waiting on the other side of the curtain.

I get dressed slowly, still feeling a little trembly. I pull open my sock drawer and before I can form a complete thought my body recoils in horror. Suddenly I'm on the floor, like I've seen a snake and am trying to get away as quickly as humanly possible.

I wish it were a snake. Snakes get into houses sometimes, snakes can climb into drawers. A snake would make sense.

None of this makes sense. There is no logical explanation.

Uncle Roderick's high school yearbook is in my sock drawer. Something spirited it there. Something opened to his senior year picture, his bright white grin, his hair with a sharp side part. There's a wheezing sound and I know it's coming from my heaving chest. I force my legs to stand, knees trembling, and drag myself forward. Stare at his face, like I'm waiting for it to say something.

Eighteen-year-olds seem so grown-up to me, but all I can think of is how young he looked, fresh and happy and full of hope. So different from the way his face was the last time I saw him, tired and sad and sagging and trying so hard to look cheerful for me.

The picture doesn't talk, of course. This isn't storybook magic. But underneath his headshot is a quotation: "'Be yourself; everyone else is already taken.'—Oscar Wilde," and I know exactly what it would sound like in his voice. A voice I'll never hear again. But a voice that—I know this now—is trying to make itself heard.

Uncle Roderick is back. Maybe never left. And is trying to talk to me.

nine

If someone had told me that I'd want to get away from my uncle, I wouldn't have believed them. But that was when I thought he was at peace. Before he started haunting me, affecting my dreams, leaving things in my room. Now all I want is some space, to figure out what to do next.

I spend the whole day outside. In every ghost story I've ever read, the ghost doesn't leave the house. Nothing scary has ever happened in a sunlit field, at least not in books. There are those woods around, but they're not dark, tangled, big bad wolf woods. Just some trees.

Every time I try to state the facts to myself—uncle, spirit, restless, back—my brain skitters away from them, latching on to whatever I'm doing that moment. "The girl roamed through the forest, wondering about the mystery in her house," I think. "She climbed a tree," I narrate, climbing a tree, "with a book gripped in her teeth, and read for hours." Or try to read, staring at sentences for minutes at a time while my mind whips between the story I'm reading and the story that's happening to me. When I pop inside for a glass of water, Mom remarks that I'm getting tan, and that she's sure the fresh air is good for me. She's spending the day holed up in her studio. Her fingers are covered in paint and glue and marker, her mouth tight.

At around four in the afternoon I'm calf-deep in cool water, thinking, "She waded in the creek looking for minnows," when I hear something. At first it's only the sound of the water, rushing over rocks and splashing onto itself, bubbling and whirlpooling. I know the phrase "babbling brook" from books, so at first it doesn't seem odd to hear a babbling sound from the water. It sounds a little like voices at first. Not people voices, just wordless chatter. But then it stops sounding like voices, and more like one voice. I don't notice right away; the creek is full of little fish and I'm trying to catch them in my hands, moving as fast as I can. But minnows are quicksilver, so I stop splashing around and stay very still, crouched with my hands cupped in the water, waiting for a fish to swim into them.

And that's when I hear it. One voice. Not a babbling brook, but a person talking. A man's voice. I can't make out any words, but it sounds like someone shouting in a house they're not sure is empty, asking if anyone is there, if anyone can hear them. Not those words, exactly, but that's the urgency I hear behind the voice I can barely make out over the rushing water and the sudden pounding in my chest. It sounds like Uncle Roderick. I slowly stand up straight, water dripping down from my fingers, and try to turn in whatever direction the voice is coming from. I strain my ears and swivel my head this way and that, but it's coming from everywhere, and nowhere.

His voice is insistent but calm, sharp but soothing. Like someone telling you to wake up, to get out, but not to panic. But none of the words are clear. I hear something like "You need to," or "I need to tell you." Maybe I hear my name. It's a voice more familiar than my own thoughts echoing in my head, but muffled, like it's coming through a wall filled with cotton and cobwebs. The voice gets louder and louder, until it's booming in my ears, but I'm not hearing it in my ears. I'm hearing it inside my *skull*. It reaches a crescendo, and I suddenly remember the only time in my life that Uncle Roderick yelled at me. I was five and nearly pulled a pot of boiling water off the stove. He sounded mad then, because he was trying to keep me safe. He sounds mad now.

The moment that thought crosses my mind, the voice begins to subside. It grows softer and softer, going from roaring timpani to a soothing whisper. Then it fades away to nothing, leaving only a headache. I don't know what he was trying to say. Is it a warning? Is he back to keep me safe from something?

I stay in the creek until I start to shiver. Hoping the voice comes back, and that I'll understand it. I don't know how long I wait, but the sun goes from high up in the sky to hovering over the horizon, and the sun sets late this time of year. It's not cold outside, but I'm standing perfectly still up to my knees in wild water, and by the time I notice that I'm a little chilly, my whole body is shaking. When I finally wade out of the creek I'm so stiff that I trip and fall, and my legs are pasty and wrinkled. I squelch home, my head still throbbing.

Once home I go straight to the bathroom and sit down on the toilet for what feels like forever. I don't know how long my bladder has been near bursting, and once I'm done it's hard to stand up again.

"Honey, are you home? Come to my studio when you're done!" I hear Mom's voice loud and clear.

"Okay!" I shout back. My voice sounds normal too. I shake my head a few times, hard, trying to reset from the weirdness of the day. When I finally get up to wash my hands I glance at myself in the medicine cabinet mirror, and the face reflected back isn't mine.

This never happened to Mom, or to Uncle Roderick. I remember being little and asking them about it. "What goes wrong with the mirrors sometimes?" is how I asked it, and they didn't understand. I tried to explain, and said something like "When your face looks wrong." They looked at each other, worried, so I never brought it up again. Whenever the strange reflection shows up I avert my eyes.

But right now I'm looking. And I can't explain what

seems so wrong, but I just know that it's a different face staring back at me. If I described it, it would sound like me: long, straight dark hair pulled back in a tight ponytail. Green-blue eyes, a tanned face with freckles. Nothing special. But that face isn't *mine*. It looks like someone's idea of what I look like, without me behind it.

I stare into the blue-green eyes, and they don't blink until I do. Maybe a sliver of a second late. I don't break eye contact until Mom shouts, "Are you okay in there?" and when I look back, the strangeness has fled and it's just my normal face again, looking tired and worried.

"One sec!" I yell back, and practice different expressions until the line between my eyebrow fades and my smile is less forced.

I bang open the door to Mom's studio. Her desk is covered with scraps of black tissue paper, white card stock, and rubber cement. "Where have you been all afternoon?" she asks. "I tried calling for you, but you must have been having adventures on the other side of the field."

"Eek, sorry. I was at the creek catching minnows." That much is true.

"That's okay. I just wanted to let you know that you might be feeding yourself tonight. Moira's mom called, she wants to take me out to dinner and talk business. I know you haven't been on your own since Roddy died, so if you want to come with, you can."

"It's okay," I say. Nothing has actually tried to hurt me, I remind myself, and Mom has barely left the house all summer. She hasn't gone out with any friends for at least a year. And besides, creepy things have been happening whether she's home or not, so she might as well have a good night.

Mom hugs me tight and kisses the top of my head. I don't know why head-kisses are such a mom thing, but I like them.

"There's leftover chicken if you want that for dinner, or make yourself some soup or macaroni and cheese. Or heck, Oreos and pretzels, if you promise not to tell me. Whatever you feel like. Watch a movie if you want to." She's putting on her shoes and straightening up her desk.

"I'll be fine, Mom!" I say. "You have fun. Tell you what, I'll make myself a well-balanced meal if you bring me back a doughnut or something." I'm amazed at how normal I sound. It must be convincing, because she laughs, kisses me on the head again, and heads out.

I make macaroni and cheese for dinner. Velveeta, not powder. So technically shells and almost-cheese, I guess. Uncle Roderick never understood why I liked it better than his fancy béchamel sauce with local cheeses. He said the bright orange "cheese product" was basically plastic. I liked his *nouilles et fromage en casserole,* like they call it in *From the Mixed-Up Files of Mrs. Basil E. Frankweiler.* But whenever he wasn't around for dinner, I would beg Mom to make Velveeta for a treat. While the water is boiling I snack on some broccoli and baby carrots, because I like broccoli and baby carrots and believe in fulfilling my promise of a balanced dinner.

I usually eat at the table, with a book, but feel like treating myself tonight. I plop down on the couch and put the steaming bowl next to me, then I switch on the TV. Velveeta is better once it's cooled off a bit and crusts. I know it's gross, but I love it. I find the cartoons channel and settle in.

I'm like some independent, self-assured character in a book, having a cozy night at home. The scene would be more picturesque in the fall or winter, with a blanket around my legs and a mug of tea or cocoa. But this is pretty nice. With the TV on, I don't feel lonely. Just alone.

I've only taken one bite when a door bangs open, way off in the distance. Doors slam themselves open and shut all the time in my house, so I don't really notice it. And I barely notice the second one slamming shut a few seconds later. But I notice the third, and the fourth, because they're getting closer, one at a time.

I'm scarcely breathing. It doesn't help. The doors slam again, in the opposite direction this time, and as the farthest-away door bangs, I hear a TV turn on upstairs, the one in Mom's room. Then the radio in the kitchen snaps on. The TV I'm watching shuts itself off. And then the house is suddenly, and completely, silent.

"Hello?" I call. "Who's there?" Like I don't know.

I'm not expecting an answer, exactly. But I have to say *something*. Uncle Roderick, or whatever is left of him, knows I'm here.

Nothing happens. I consider getting up, walking around, seeing if there are any messages written in fog on a window or scrawled onto a mirror. I swing my legs down off the couch, but before I can stand up, everything happens at once.

The TV turns itself on again, volume up as high as it gets, and flips through channels at a dizzying pace. I hear the radio in the kitchen do the same, and the TV in Mom's room. But then, I can barely hear them over the racket of what must be every door in the house banging open and shut, open and shut, hard enough to fling them off their hinges. I know Mom locked the front door, but that one is slamming too, and so is the sliding glass door behind me, and even the windows are flinging open and shut, open and shut, gusting freezing cold air through the warm room even though it's still summer-hot outside. The bowl of shells and cheese next to me flings itself off the couch cushion, shattering onto the floor, scattering pasta everywhere.

I don't know what to do. All I can think of is to flip over and press my face into the corner of the couch like a little kid, believing that if I can't see someone in a game of hide-and-seek, they can't see me. I put my arms over my head and scream into the cushions until my ears are ringing.

Is this what Uncle Roderick wants? Does he want me to be afraid? I don't believe that, but my whole body is stiff with terror, this can't be happening but it *is* and all I want is for it to be over.

It ends slowly. One at a time the devices switch off. The doors stop banging and start swaying, I hear their latches clicking in and out of place until they settle open or closed. The windows stay open, and the deadbolt thunks into the front door again. The TV in front of me flips back through the channels until it lands on the cartoons I was watching.

I slowly pull myself out of the couch cushions, panting and sweating. As I sit up, the volume on the cartoons slides up and down a little, until it's perfect. It's confusing. Like it (he) wants to take care of me, after scaring the crickets out of me. Like it's (he's) saying *I'm sorry for scaring you, it's okay, you're okay*. My dinner is still on the floor, the bowl still broken, but other than that everything is back to normal.

By the time Mom gets home I'm still shaky, but have myself mostly together. The floor is clean. The pieces of broken bowl are buried deep in the trash can. I forced myself to check upstairs and nothing looked wrong there. She kisses my head, gives me a glossy brown paper bag, and asks how my night went. I tell her it was fine.

She looks worried anyway. "How was dinner?" I ask. I peek in the bag, it's a chocolate glazed doughnut. My favorite.

Mom sits down gingerly on the other end of the couch,

tossing her bag on the floor. She pulls a throw pillow onto her lap and picks at the embroidery; it's one that I remember Uncle Roderick working on as we watched old movies together. A light blue-and-white paisley pattern.

"I'm not going to lie to you, sweetheart. It wasn't great. There's just so much more competition than there used to be. When we first got started, stores would fill an entire spinning rack with our cards. Now we're lucky if we get one side. Ellen likes some of the new designs, but she says that vendors will order those instead of older products, not in addition to them."

"Oh." I'm holding the bag with the doughnut so tightly it crinkles. I'm not even hungry. I wish I hadn't asked her to get me one, and hope it didn't cost much. "What . . . what does that mean? For us? And for Moira's family?" There, now I don't sound so self-centered.

She holds the throw pillow tight against her body, hugging it. I know I should hug her, but I can't. I remember the morning Uncle Roderick died, me comforting her, and how it felt good and wrong at the same time. "Moira's family is fine," she says. "Remember, her dad has his architecture business, it's going very well. This area is having a lot of new development, believe it or not. As for us . . . well, it's too early to say. Maybe it will be an opportunity. This house always was too big for just three people. It's definitely too big for two."

She's not talking about selling the house. She can't be

saying that we would move. Uncle Roderick is in the garden and the woods and the creek, and some of his ashes might still be floating in the wind. We can't leave him now. That can't be what she's saying. There's that skin-crawling sensation of someone standing right behind me. No, several someones. The Patersons, my uncle, whoever else lived and died here. Everyone we'd be leaving. We can't abandon them.

"Maybe we could open a bed-and-breakfast," I say. "Or take in boarders. Lodgers." I like that idea, running a boardinghouse. Or an artist retreat. Any book about a girl living in a house like that would be a good one.

"Maybe," Mom says. I sag back into the couch, a little bit of tension draining out of me. I'm even lightheaded and take a deep breath for the first time in what might be hours.

"Let's not worry about it yet, sweetheart. Nothing will change right away. And we'll talk a lot, about whatever comes down the pike." She stretches, yawns. "I know our conversation couldn't possibly get any more cheerful, but take a look at this book Ellen gave me." She rummages through her bag, pulls out a book with a pastel green-and-yellow cover. She tosses it across the couch to me. It lands upside down, but if I crane my neck I can read the spine.

" '*On Death and Dying*,' ". I read aloud. "Fun. Like a how-to guide?"

"Ha. Kind of. Not how to die, but about how to get through it when someone else dies."

"Hm." I pick it up because I can tell she wants me to, and flip through it.

Mom scooches so she's sitting next to me, breaks off a chunk of my untouched doughnut and pops it into her mouth while pointing to a page. "She talks about how there are stages of grief you move through. Denial, anger, bargaining, depression, and acceptance."

I move my finger down the page, looking at each one. "Are you in denial?" I ask. Mom shakes her head. "Anger?" She shakes her head again.

"What about you?" she asks. "Bargaining?"

"I don't think so," I say. There probably isn't a chapter called "How to Handle the Death of a Loved One When They're Still Haunting You." I put my finger down between "depression" and "acceptance."

"I'm probably here?" I guess. "I don't know if I went through those other things. He was sick too long for there to be much denial. Or anger. We probably got those out of the way early." I remember my doughnut and take a bite. It's too doughy, and turns into paste in my mouth. I swallow hard, and put the rest in the bag.

"That's very sensible and efficient of us," says Mom. "And I'm right there with you, sweetheart. I'm not sure why Ellen wanted me to read this, but it's nice that she's trying to help. Is the doughnut okay?"

"It's great," I lie. "I'm saving it for later. I'm still full from dinner. Velveeta. And some vegetables."

Mom smiles, a real one, gathering me into a hug. I hug her back, a normal good-night hug. Not an "I don't want to leave this house" hug. Not an "I'm being haunted" hug. An "everything is fine, no need to worry about your daughter" hug. We hold each other for a little longer than usual, and then turn in for the night.

In bed, wide awake, eyes clenched tight against whatever I might see lurking there in the dark, I run through what I know.

Uncle Roderick died, but something is wrong. He isn't resting peacefully. I don't know why. He's trying to get my attention—dreams, notes, and now this larger disturbance. He needs to tell me something, but I don't know what. And there's one place left to look for answers.

ten

The next morning I'm groggy. No dreams, luckily. Or maybe it's not luck, maybe Uncle Roderick knows that I'm going to find out what's going on, why he hasn't left yet, and so he doesn't need to tap into my subconscious to give me messages. I yawn through breakfast and then hop on my bike.

I haven't ridden into town all summer. There's not much to do there besides go to the library, and I haven't been in the mood for new books. But that's where I'm going to find some information.

It's a long ride. Our driveway is a gravel road a mile long, thick with trees on all sides. The street we officially live off, Sullivan Road, is hard-packed dirt. I wonder what it's like to have neighbors.

Every pump of my legs on the pedals brings me that much farther away from my house. My breath comes fast, my heart pounds. From exertion instead of fear, for a change. I haven't been this far from home since that day at Moira's, and since then I've been outside, avoiding my house, or inside and having bad dreams and dealing with them. Breathing hard, pedaling fast, trees blurring past me, I'm more relaxed than I have been in a long time. I've never had the urge to get away from something before, and never understood how much relief it could bring.

The book Mom brought home pops into my mind. I like the idea that there are stages of grief you can move through, in a nice and orderly way that ends with acceptance. I also wonder if this whole ghost thing is a kind of bargaining. Like, Uncle Roderick making some bargain with the universe, or with the afterlife. He's allowed to stay a little longer because . . . well, I don't know why yet. That's what I have to find out.

Or maybe I'm bargaining. Maybe I'm keeping him here, somehow, because I don't want to let him go. If I was really at acceptance, then he'd be able to rest in peace.

But, no. It can't be my fault that part of him is still here. He has to know that I just want him to be okay, and if he can't be okay and alive, I want him to be okay with being dead. Even if it means leaving us behind, forever.

I'll figure it out. Half an hour of riding and I'm at the library. I push open the doors and inhale deeply as the air-conditioning washes over me. I hadn't noticed how hot I was until now, but my faded black T-shirt is sticking to my chest, and my forehead is damp with sweat. Mrs. Goldman, the librarian, waves at me as I come in, and I wave back before going over to the computer. I come here all the time during the school year, sometimes on my own, sometimes with my mom or my uncle. Mrs. Goldman moved here from New York City too, so they would chat about that a lot. She was one of the people I couldn't bring myself to speak to at the wake.

I type a few keywords into the catalog: "Ghost," "Haunted," "Supernatural," write down a few call numbers, and meander over to the stacks, stopping at a few shelves along the way so anyone watching won't see me make an anxious beeline for that section. The library is mostly empty so I don't know what prying eyes I'm afraid of, but you never know who might be peering at you from between the shelves.

Once I've aimlessly wandered over to the exact section I need, I pull out a stack of titles that look helpful. One is like an encyclopedia of the supernatural, another is about ghost sightings around the world. A few other books that might be too similar to help but still could be useful. I carry them over to a table tucked into a corner, set them down with a satisfying *thump,* and settle in to read.

I've always loved ghost stories, but have only ever read fiction. Some "based on a true story," but everything I know about ghosts is from folktales and chapter books and movies. It never seemed important to research the different presences in my house, any more than it felt necessary to learn about the different woods that make up the doors and the roof and the kitchen table. But that was before one of them tried to get my attention.

Two hours later, I still don't know for sure why Uncle Roderick is haunting me, but I have a slightly better idea.

There is the possibility that it's not actually the ghost of my uncle. It could also be a poltergeist, which literally means "noisy spirit." They're a type of ghost known for slamming doors, breaking mirrors, throwing knickknacks or books or even furniture around a room. I read a bunch of descriptions of poltergeists, and it sounds a lot like what's been happening at home. Also, apparently they can be caused by extreme distress inside a person, especially a young person.

I'm a young person. And I guess losing Uncle Roderick counts as distress. But I'm not convinced that it's a poltergeist, because usually everyone in a house knows when there's one poltering around, and Mom hasn't noticed anything at all. I didn't read any accounts of poltergeists only poltering one person. Like a target.

"Excuse me, dear," a voice says, and my whole body convulses in surprise. I was so absorbed in research that I didn't notice the librarian coming over.

"Oh sorry, is it time to close up?" My voice is a little shaky.

"No, not quite yet, and I'm so sorry to startle you. But

there's a new boy in town, he's come to visit the library several times and I thought he might like to meet another young person."

And there is someone behind her. A boy, around my age, blond hair and hazel eyes, exactly as tanned as me. The kid Moira heard about, who moved into the Baumlers' old farmhouse? He's wearing plaid shorts and a bright white T-shirt, and suddenly I feel extremely grubby. I'm not used to meeting new kids, but I stand up from my chair and stick out my hand for him to shake.

"My name's Griffin," he says as Mrs. Goldman walks away.

"I'm Bug," I tell him. He cocks his head in surprise at my name but doesn't say anything about it, which I like. We sit down at the table, books spread across it.

"We just moved here from Portland," he says. "My parents used to be lawyers, but they both hated it. We moved into some old farmhouse, my mom is writing a novel and my dad is figuring out how chickens and goats and things work. It's okay. I'm pretty sure our house is haunted, though."

"Perfect!" I exclaim. He looks confused, which makes sense—that's not a normal thing to say. I hasten to explain. "My house is haunted too. That's why I came to the library, why I have all these books. I want to learn more about ghosts." One specific ghost, really, but I don't tell him that. Believing in ghosts is one thing, but explaining to this total stranger that my dead uncle has come back to tell me something is probably a little too much.

"Oh!" He laughs with a flash of purple braces. "That is kinda perfect. Have you learned anything good?"

"A lot. First, ghosts don't haunt people for no reason. Sometimes it's because a person died in a way that left something of them behind. And now a little bit of their energy is still stuck doing something, over and over. Those hauntings only happen because you're in a place where something bad happened to someone."

I cringe for a second, worried that I'm coming off as abnormally obsessed, but Griffin just nods thoughtfully. "Could that explain weird sounds? Like someone walking up and down stairs?"

"Definitely," I say. For a second I wonder where this Bug, who's talking so confidently to some strange boy, came from. But ghosts make sense to me, and Griffin seems happy to listen, so I barrel ahead. "If there are any random cold spots that never warm up, that's why. This all explains a lot of the random ghostly things that have happened in my house since forever."

"But there are other kinds of ghosts too, right? That do things on purpose?" Griffin is flipping through one of the books now, stopping at a photograph with a white splotch hovering behind a grinning toddler.

"Yeah." There's a prickling down the back of my neck. It's

fun to talk about, but this is real for me. It might be real for him too. "Sometimes ghosts haunt people into doing things. Or because there's something that person needs to know. Like avenging their death. Or solving a mystery. Or passing along a message." I find the chapter I was reading and pass it over to him.

"'Those hauntings sometimes mimic a poltergeist,'" Griffin reads out loud, "'and can manifest in a variety of ways. Witnesses have observed objects floating, or breaking dramatically.' Sounds scary."

"Yeah," I say. "I'm glad I've never seen anything like *that*, yikes."

Griffin continues to look through the book, pointing at another paragraph. "It also says that these types of hauntings are usually *localized*, which means they only happen in one place, but they can also follow a person around. I wonder if there are any at the library?" he asks, looking around dramatically.

I look under the table, which makes him laugh. "Ghost-free!" I exclaim, but the memory of the voice in the creek ripples through my mind. We both pore over our books for a while. It's a companionable quiet, though, like we've already gotten close enough to not have to talk.

For a moment it feels okay, like we're just two kids looking at books, but then that narrator in my head starts describing the scene, a girl in ratty clothes sitting across from this new boy, who is objectively cute, and where any normal story might go from there. I tell myself that I'm being ridiculous, I barely know him, but I can't focus on the words in front of me because I'm suddenly convinced that everything about me, my hair, my clothes, is completely wrong compared to this boy, who is effortlessly right in the same way Moira is an effortlessly right girl. I have to go before he realizes that everything is wrong with me, and am frantically casting about for an excuse to run away when he points to a page and says, "Hey, this is interesting!"

"What?" I say, trying to sound like I didn't just invent something to panic about.

"According to this, the first kind of ghost—the trapped-energy kind—can stick around forever. Just doing the same things, like an endless loop. The second kind, the ones that want to pass a message along, can't stick around forever. They're drawn to the afterlife, but force themselves to stay here to finish whatever it is they need to finish. The longer they stick around, the more . . . stretched, it seems like? they become, between this world and the next."

Oh no. I have so many questions, but if I sound too worried Griffin will wonder why. How long do I have? What happens if Uncle Roderick gets stuck here? What if he gets pulled away before I figure this out?

"The library is closing in ten minutes!" calls Mrs. Goldman, and I jump. Is it almost six o'clock already? I hope Mom isn't wondering what happened to me.

Griffin pulls a phone out of his pocket and looks at the screen. "My mom is waiting outside. I want to check out this book first, though!" My heart sinks a little. That was the only one I had wanted to take out. I need it more than him. But "I can help you clean up," he continues, "she won't mind waiting. She's been wanting me to make new friends."

A bubbly sensation rises through my chest. Who is this boy, who just says things like that? Just assumes that someone would want to be his friend? Is that how people make friends, by believing that it's possible, even likely? I try to smile in a way that looks normal and friendly and not completely flabbergasted. "That's okay!" I say. "I took them out, I can put them back. But maybe I'll see you around. We could do something. Or something." We could do something, or something. Brilliant, Bug.

He smiles. "Cool. You want to put my number in your phone?"

Crap. "I don't have a phone. I mean, my house does. I don't. I'll probably get one before middle school starts, though." That probably isn't true, but it could happen. Is he going to think I'm some old-fashioned weirdo? I *am* an old-fashioned weirdo, I guess, but he doesn't need to know that right away.

"No worries, I'll write it down for you," he says, like it's no big deal. He grabs a piece of scrap paper and a pencil while Mrs. Goldman checks out his book, scribbles down a name and number, and waves goodbye.

Well. That was unexpected, but nice. I fold up the paper and stick it in my pocket, then pile up the stack of books and bring them back to the section. I put them away, one at a time, enjoying the rasp of cover against cover. As I'm walking out of the aisle a loud *thump* comes from behind me. I turn, and one of the books I just put away is lying on the floor.

It's the one that taught me about ghosts passing along messages. About how they only haunt the living if they have something they need to communicate. I know I put it away right. It wouldn't fall on its own. "Okay, okay," I say out loud. "I get it." I slide the book back, and it stays this time. I don't need to check it out, because I already know what it's trying to tell me.

This isn't one of the normal stages of grief. I have to figure out what Uncle Roderick wants from me.

eleven

I bike over to Moira's house the next day. I didn't have any dreams worth remembering last night, which tells me that I'm on the right path toward figuring this out.

Griffin's number is still in my shorts. There must be some rule about how long I should wait before calling him, but I don't know what that rule is. Moira would know. And I should probably tell her that I met the kid from the old Baumler place, but I don't want to because she'd probably start acting like he's my future boyfriend, or her future boyfriend, and I don't even want to think about that sort of thing.

I don't think about boys like that. I don't think about boys much at all, to be honest. It takes a lot of work to figure out how to do "girl" the right way, and of course I've wondered if I would get along better with boys. Some of the tougher girls in school hang out with the different boy groups. But they all play football at recess and shove each other, and I hate sports. One group of boys and girls always spend their free time playing some complicated game with a lot of rules about dragons and wizards, but that isn't my thing either. That's why I just read during free time.

Still. I know she would want to hear about Griffin, but now's not the time. We need to focus.

I pull up to her house, and Moira's already sitting on the porch. We probably should practice not hanging out, but I need her help.

I take off my backpack and pull out a thin, narrow black box, the letters *O-U-I-J-A* stamped in flaky gold on the side. I had told her over the phone that I wanted to try to contact Uncle Roderick. I didn't say why. I didn't have to, because why wouldn't I want to talk to him? We've played with this Ouija board before, trying to reach her grandmother, my dad, Abraham Lincoln, and Judy Garland. We usually got gibberish, sometimes words that didn't make any sense. But it's going to work this time. It has to.

We sit cross-legged on the floor of the porch. A shiver goes up my spine. I had always thought this was a harmless game, fun for creeping ourselves out but not really real. But one of the books I read yesterday had said that Ouija boards can be dangerous. That they can open you up to other worlds, and invite spirits into ours. And while I'm not sure how Moira will react if we get a real message from Uncle Roderick, that book had said that playing with a Ouija board by yourself is one of the most dangerous things you can do. You need another person there to form a protective circle. Or something. I actually stopped reading after that because I got too scared. I'm just going to assume that everything will turn out okay.

Moira's eyes are narrowed with focus, her shoulders hunched forward. Both our arms are stretched out, fingertips barely touching the lightweight pale planchette. (I didn't know it was called a planchette until I read about Ouija boards in one of the library books. I'm not exactly sure what the word "planchette" means. Probably not "little plastic doohickey.")

I'm sitting as still as I can, my whole body tense and ready. And then the planchette starts to move.

"*S . . . Q . . . T . . . N . . . I . . . L . . . M*," Moira spells out slowly, tracking the letters it pauses on. "Squat nilm? What's a squat nilm? Is it like a kumquat?"

"I don't know. You must be moving it."

"No I'm not! You are!"

"Maybe we both are," I say, trying not to sound disappointed. "Let's try again."

I take a few deep breaths, trying to calm my thudding heart. When the planchette got going I was thrilled, but as one nonsense letter follows another the butterflies in my stomach turn to dragonflies. Or something else, jagged and fast. Moira tries to breathe with me but keeps erupting into giggles. I glare at her, and she slowly gets herself under control.

"Okay. Okay. Sorry. Let's try again."

Deep breaths. I close my eyes. A mild summer wind against my cheeks. A trickle of sweat down my forehead, my hair sweaty and hot against my neck. I lift my hand from the planchette for a second to tug my ponytail back. *Talk to me,* I plead, silently. *Please?*

I don't move the planchette. Neither does Moira. Neither does anything else. It stays still as a stone. As a doornail, I think, when a burst of light erupts behind my eyelids and an earsplitting crash rips a scream from my throat.

Moira jumps up from the floor. "Thunderstorm!" she hollers. While we had been sitting there, eyes closed, the sky had gone from blue to grayish orange and opened up like an envelope. Bullet-like rain bounces off the porch roof. The planchette is upside down and off to the side; one of us must have flipped it by accident.

Moira runs into the backyard. She loves huge storms, always has. I hate the way wet clothes hang down my back and arms, the waistband tight and scratchy. I envy her abandon. I want to run out there with her, cool off, feel as free and alive as Moira looks with her arms out, spinning in circles. But I didn't bring a change of clothes with me, and don't want to wear any of hers. I stretch my bare legs and feet out from under the porch roof, let the rain bathe them. That's enough. It has to be enough.

But it's not enough for Moira. "Come *on*, Bug!" she shouts.

I shake my head, but she dashes to the porch, pulls me up by my arms, and drags me out with her. I'm instantly soaked through to the skin. I hunch my shoulders and shiver. My shirt presses down on me, like those lead aprons you wear to get X-rays at the dentist. But I can't get any wetter. It won't get any worse. So when Moira grabs my hands and starts spinning in circles with me, I let her. Some of her joy passes on to me and soon I'm smiling, then laughing, as we whirl faster and faster under the ominous sky. It's like the fleeting moments we had together when we were small and not fighting, and I suddenly wish our whole friendship looked like this moment, quick and free.

Like most late July storms, this one stops as quickly as it started. By the time we squelch our way back to the porch the sun is shining through the clouds, glinting tiny rainbows off the grass.

"That was fun," she says. "Thanks for coming out with me. I'm way cooler now!"

"And a lot more drippy," I say, and pretend to shake myself like a dog.

"Worth it," she retorts. She squeezes excess water out of her summer dress, stomps her feet, and goes inside. I do the same, but it's harder to wring water out of denim. Both her parents are out, so there's no one to tell us not to track water through their fancy house. We go straight up to her room, and she immediately strips off her dress before getting a new one out of the closet. I avert my eyes, staring at her bookshelf intently even though it hasn't changed in years. We used to undress in front of each other all the time, at slumber parties, getting ready to go to the lake, but it's different now. I thought it was part of getting older, but she still doesn't seem to mind. Maybe it's just another weird thing about me, another part of getting older that I haven't figured out yet.

"Here," she calls, and before I'm ready she flings a dress at me. It hits me in the face, but I manage to catch it before it falls to the floor.

"Thanks," I say. I want to ask if she has an extra pair of shorts and a spare T-shirt, instead of this dress. But I don't want to ask. It's not a big deal, right?

I take off my shorts and shirt. They puddle around my feet, damp and cold. I slip the dress on over my head and it fits me perfectly. Clings a little around my middle, then flares out around my hips and thighs. It's a pale blue, with yellow splotches scattered randomly. It's pretty. I've never seen it before; Moira must have bought it with her mom earlier in the summer.

It's very comfortable. More comfortable than my normal outfits, if I'm being honest. Softer, without constriction around the waist. I bet it's more breezy too, and easier to climb trees in.

"You look good," says Moira. I look up, and she's staring at me approvingly. "It fits you perfectly. You should dress like that more often. If you want we can go to the mall sometime, I bet one of our moms will drive us. I can help you pick out more."

"Thanks," I say. I'm not sure about that, though. I look like an entirely different person from the neck down. I look like a real girl. But my head still feels the same, like myself. A Bug's head floating above a girl's body. I mean, it always feels that way, because I *am* a girl. So my head is always floating over a girl's body. But I can't stop staring down at myself. It's like I'm a paper doll, this cut-out blue dress stuck onto me with paper tabs. Or a drag queen, without the wig and makeup. It looks good, and makes my stomach hurt. Not like the dragonflies are back. Not quite like a stone, either. More like I've swallowed my bike chain. Greasy and cold, rising up into the back of my throat, making me shudder.

"Want to watch a movie?" Moira asks. I shrug, or nod, or something, and we head to the kitchen to load up on snacks before settling down.

Her head is in the pantry, but her voice comes out clearly. "I'm sorry we didn't hear from your uncle," she says.

I tug open the refrigerator and look through the vegetable crisper. Baby carrots are good. "It's okay," I say. Is there ever anything else to say when someone says they're sorry?

"What . . ." She pauses for a second, like she's not sure she wants to ask, but then forges ahead. "What did you want him to say?" She pulls out some packets of dried fruit and nuts. Neither of us is a popcorn person.

"I don't know," I say, which is true. I have no idea what he's trying to tell me. But Moira is quiet, like she's waiting for me to keep going. I have to say something. "Maybe . . . maybe that he's okay. That he's not hurting anymore, that he's happy wherever he is and we can stop being sad."

Moira moves next to me and takes two bottles of ginger ale, pressing one into my hand. "That might be true anyway," she says softly. She's not looking at me, but there's a tenderness to her voice, her movements. "Like, whether he tells you that or not."

I wish it were true, but I know it's not. Not yet. My eyes prickle, but I will not cry in front of Moira. Especially not in this dress. "I know," I lie in a whisper. "But it would still be nice to hear."

Moira squeezes my shoulder, and we carry our snacks into the living room. She picks a movie and asks if I want to see it. I say yes, even though I wasn't paying attention. I don't catch the title and can't follow the plot, and Moira keeps glancing at me like she wants to talk more, but I can't. As soon as it's over I leave.

twelve

I bike toward home still wearing Moira's dress. She said I could keep it. "The color matches your complexion more than mine," she had explained, and went on to tell me about undertones, cool and warm, and what mine is compared to hers. I don't remember which mine is. I wonder if the dress is expensive, if it's one my mom could afford to buy me, if taking it will help us save some money. My backpack, stuffed with my wet clothes and the Ouija board, bumps against my shoulder blades as if saying *hello again, hello again*.

Biking in a dress is more pleasant than I expected. It bunches easily underneath the seat, and my legs are free. The air rushes past them, strong and cool. Every time I look down I think, "There's a girl riding this bike. That girl is me. I'm a girl riding a bike." When I wear my regular clothes I focus on the road or where I'm going to or drift into a million different daydreams, but this is different. It's like whooshing downhill, very fast, even though this stretch of road is pretty flat. There's still a bike chain coiled up inside my gut, and I start to wonder if it's something I ate. Then

I remember that I didn't eat anything during the movie except for a few baby carrots. I just have to ignore it till it goes away.

I'm still so disappointed in the failed Ouija session, and wish I knew how much time we have before Uncle Roderick stops being able to communicate. That book Griffin checked out could tell me. And I realize, he gave me his number but I also know where he lives. The Baumler farmhouse isn't exactly on the way home from Moira's, but it's not too far away. Not on a bike. So I veer left where I would usually veer right and zip toward his house, blue-and-yellow dress fluttering around me.

While pedaling I imagine what I'll say. I'll be standing on his front porch, taller somehow, beautiful in my dress, hair still a little wet but that just makes it look darker and shinier. "Just thought I'd pop by," I'll say breezily, and talk about how *interesting* that book sounds, if I could just borrow it for a bit, and he'll be so charmed and impressed that he'll give it to me and I'll find out everything. And Griffin will think I'm a cool, pretty girl with just the right amount of mystery.

This whole scenario is running through my head as I pull up to his house and get off my bike. My dress catches over the seat and I almost fall into a heap on the lawn but free myself before that happens. I ring the doorbell and hear footsteps come down the hall. The door opens and there's Griffin in front of me, as perfectly put together as yesterday, and suddenly the opening speech I've been rehearsing falls out of my mouth in a heap.

"I popped by!" is what I say. "Because, of that interesting book? From yesterday, and I know you gave me your number but I know where you live, not because I know where *you* live but. I mean, I know you moved into this house, and I know where this house is, and—"

He's looking at me, smiling, a little confused. This is all going so wrong. He looks down at my dress and I suddenly realize how dressy it is, how wrong it looks on me right now, like showing up to a country fair in a ball gown, and the bike chain in my stomach coils around itself like a snake ready to strike.

"Do you want to come in?" he asks.

I take a deep breath and try to go back to the beginning. Ignore everything else, just get the right words out. "Sorry. What I meant to say is, I just wanted to stop by for a second. I was curious about that book you checked out yesterday, do you mind if I borrow it for a little bit? I promise that I'm very responsible with library books, and if anything happens to it I can explain it to Mrs. Goldman, she's known me my whole life." There, that sounds normal. That sounds like the person he wanted to be friends with.

"Oh!" he says. "Sure! I can grab it, but *do* you want to come in?"

I think about all the terrible wrong things I could say, sitting on his couch, dress draped neatly across my thighs, and feel like I'm going to throw up. "I have to get going," is what I say instead. "My mom will be home soon, she'll worry if I'm not back."

That must sound reasonable, so he disappears inside his house for a second and trots back with the book. "Come over again soon and we can talk about it!" he exclaims.

"Sure," I say, shoving it into my backpack, a little shocked to be invited back but maybe he's just saying that to be nice. "What I meant earlier, also, about knowing where you live? It's just, we knew that a new family had moved into the Baumler farmhouse. And of course I knew where that house was, I know most places in this town. So that's how I knew where you lived even though you didn't give me your address. I didn't stalk you or anything."

He grins, and my stomach settles just a little. "I figured!" he said. "Ever since we moved here people have referred to 'the Baumler farmhouse.' I think everyone knows my address. I wonder how long before they start calling it 'the Rivera farmhouse'?"

"Maybe if you and your family stay here for two hundred years," I tell him. "It's that kind of place."

"I like a challenge," he says, and we both laugh and I say goodbye.

On the ride home I avoid thinking about what I look like in a dress. Instead, I go over the conversation in my head, like each part, the initial blurt, the recovery, the friendly goodbye, are pieces of a spell that can transform me into someone who can successfully talk to a new friend. It's a spell I can only use on someone who doesn't already know me, someone who doesn't have strange, off-by-a-beat Bug to compare to. I can only change so much in Moira's eyes; she's known me too long. But now there's a twinkle of hope that she's right, that middle school can be different. That *I* can be different.

Mom's car is gone when I get home. I'm glad. I don't want her to see me dressed like this. She'll probably tell me how nice I look, and that makes me nervous. I told Moira we could go shopping sometime, but I still haven't decided for real if I'm going to dress like this in middle school. When I first saw myself, I thought I could, but what if I start feeling weird like at Griffin's house, seven thousand times a day? I don't have to decide now, but the first day of school is only a month or so away. I push my way inside the house and the door is heavier than usual. Like it doesn't want to let me in.

A lot of books have a moral, some lesson about how you have to stay true to who you are. How it doesn't matter if you're different, you don't have to act like everyone else, and that the most important thing is to be yourself. But those books never tell you how to figure out what your self is. They assume that you know already, and are pretending to be someone else for a while to fit in.

I don't know what my self is, though. Maybe that's true

for everyone. Maybe no one is really sure of who they are. I probably have to try out a bunch of different selves until I find one that fits.

Maybe being a girl in pretty dresses will fit once I get used to it. Mom doesn't dress up very much, but I think she would if she had the opportunity. I bet she'd like having a daughter she can dress up with. And Uncle Roderick loved pretty dresses. He had a lot of them. We could have dressed up together, both of us like drag queens. Well, him as a drag queen and me as a . . . just a girl. I bet he would have loved me in them.

Being around Griffin, just for a few minutes, felt like I was practicing how to be a better version of myself. It needs work, but maybe if I practice often enough it will start to feel natural. Maybe it will stop being something I have to practice, and something I'll just be. Maybe that's what growing up is like. Practice makes a person.

Once inside, I drop my backpack near the front door and kick off my shoes. I tug out the bag with wet clothes and take them into the bathroom, draping my shirt and shorts over the tub. Then I slowly, purposefully turn toward the mirror, but avoid my face. I stare at the expanse of skin that goes from the top of the dress up past my collarbone. It looks like those girls in magazines, and my stomach twists harder. When I go to get my backpack it's toppled over, and the Ouija board is sitting on the floor next to it.

I stare at it for a minute. When I took out the plastic bag

with my clothes, I know I left the zipper mostly closed. My backpack could have fallen over by itself, but there's no way the game box could have slid all the way out.

"Yeah, yeah, I get it," I say out loud. Just in case Uncle Roderick is watching. I think this means he wants me to use the Ouija board by myself. A prickle of fear creeps up my neck at the idea, but I shake it off. I'm more curious than afraid, though sometimes those feel like the same thing. I take the board upstairs to my bedroom, and it's probably my imagination, but I think it's humming in my hands.

The blue-and-yellow dress tents over my knees. Cross-legged again, the board in front of me, I place the planchette at the top, in the center. Right over the word "Ouija," whatever that means. My fingertips resting on the planchette as lightly as possible, I close my eyes and inhale deeply. I briefly consider the warning against using Ouija boards on your own, but dismiss it. My uncle will protect me.

Before I can breathe out, the plastic piece starts moving, and my eyes snap open. This is nothing like the vague meanderings I'd felt before, whenever Moira and I had played. We would pretend it was moving by itself but knew it was just our subconscious guiding it for a little bit of excitement.

But this feels real. It moves purposefully from letter to letter, tugging and pushing and guiding, and I'm convinced that if I twitched my pointer finger the tiniest bit I'd graze against another hand sharing the space with mine. So I don't. I'm frozen, my hands petrified, pulled along like a fish on a hook.

Too late, I realize that I haven't been paying attention to the letters. When Moira and I play, the planchette moves so slowly that it's easy to track the letters, to write them down and figure out where the words separate (when we've been lucky enough to get words). And we usually ask questions, so there's some context for the answers. But the plastic triangle is spinning from letter to letter so quickly that I can't figure out what words they add up to, and anyway I haven't even asked a question, so I don't know what it's trying to tell me.

"Slow down!" I cry out. Immediately it stops moving. I'm breathing hard, my heart pounding faster than it did biking up the hill.

Okay, Bug. You can do this. First things first. "Is that you, Uncle Roderick?"

The planchette shoots to "Yes," and an overwhelming weightlessness washes through me. Like I could fly up to the ceiling, I'm so happy. I want to tell him that I love him, that I miss him. That nothing is the same without him. But he must know that already.

"Is there something you want to tell me?" I didn't know I wanted to cry, but my voice is thick with tears. I push them down.

It stays at "Yes," but maybe quivers a bit.

"What is it?" Too late I realize that maybe I don't want to know. If he tells me, then that means he'll be done here.

And leave, forever this time. I screw up my eyes as the planchette starts to move, slower now, but I can't handle not knowing. And I don't want to be the reason why he's not at peace.

"*B . . . Y . . .*" By? By what?

"*O . . . U . . . R . . .*" By our . . . by our house?

"*S . . . E . . . L . . . F.*"

By ourself? "What does that mean?"

The nine letters repeat themselves. "By ourself? Yeah, Mom and I are by ourselves now. Is that what you wanted to tell me?"

The letters repeat themselves, again. Maybe more emphatically this time? He wants me to understand, but I don't, not yet.

"Are you trying to apologize for leaving us?" My voice cracks on the word "leaving." A few tears roll down my cheeks. "It's okay, Uncle Roderick. We know you didn't want to. It's not your fault." He did everything he could to stay with us. After months of treatments and drug trials and ups and downs, we spent those last days telling him it was okay to let go, to be at peace.

The planchette shoots to "No." Then it starts moving again. Slower this time. And weaker. Like the invisible hand guiding it is getting tired.

"*W . . . H . . . O . . .*"

"*A . . . R . . . E . . .*"

"*Y...O...U...*"

"Who are you? It's me, Uncle Roderick. Bug." The library books said that spirits, especially of the recently deceased, get confused a lot. Which is why they resort to bangings and crashings—it's an easy way to make themselves known and doesn't need, like, precise wording. But I'm a little worried. Does he not recognize me anymore?

"It's me," I repeat. "Your niece. Bug."

The planchette shoots back to "No." But it feels like he wants me to try again, not that he's disagreeing. Now the planchette is dragging along the board, moving as slowly as it does when it's just my subconscious guiding it.

"*B...U...*" It stops. I wait for it to move again. Is he spelling out my name? I nudge it in the direction of the *G*, but it doesn't budge.

"*B-U*," I say out loud. The planchette spins in a slow circle. I repeat the letters again, and then realize. "Oh! Be you? Is that what you're telling me?"

Slower than an inchworm the planchette pulls itself to the "Yes," then stops. I sense the invisible hand leave, and the planchette starts to tremble under my fingers. Uncle Roderick might still be hovering, too tired to communicate anymore. One of the books said that it takes a lot of energy for spirits to interact with the physical world, and I guess Uncle Roderick is tapped out. I grab a pen and some paper and scribble down everything I can remember. I wish I had been paying better attention when he first started talking to me, but all I write down is "By ourself," "Who are you," and "Be you."

I grab the library book and look for the part Griffin was talking about, but it's maddeningly brief. And general. It does say that the energy a dead person leaves behind, in the form of a "spiritual impression," or ghost, can try and contact the living. And that their energy starts to "dissipate" after some amount of time. But it doesn't say how much time. Or what happens if they fail to pass along their message. It also claims that if a ghost is trying to get in touch with you, it might be trying to avert a disaster. Or communicate a secret. Or give you advice. But it doesn't say anything about how, exactly, to figure that out.

I wonder if Uncle Roderick is trying to say the same thing Moira's been telling me all summer. That I have to get myself in some kind of order before middle school. That I have to pick what kind of person I'm going to be.

Or maybe he's trying to tell me something about himself. Like, something that he couldn't tell us before he died. Or a mistake he made when he was my age, one he doesn't want me to repeat.

I'm getting closer to figuring this out. I can tell. And I know what I have to do next.

thirteen

All the doors in our house are old, solid wood and heavy. I have a crystal clear memory of being three or four and trying to get into Uncle Roderick's room. I remember pushing hard against the door, arms straight out, every tiny muscle straining against the thick slab of oak. I started crying, because I was too young to understand and thought that maybe that door would be closed forever. It wasn't, of course. He opened it right away and scooped me up in a hug.

Today the door is as light as cardboard. I barely touch it, and it swings smoothly open. Like the room wants me to come inside. If there are any answers to why Uncle Roderick isn't resting properly, they'll be in here.

I take a deep breath before stepping across the threshold. His presence is everywhere, but I don't know if it's his ghost or just my memories. I haven't been in his room since before he died. It looks the same, but cleaner. He used to pull out whatever accumulated in his pockets over the course of the day and pile it on his nightstand, but now his nightstand is bare. He hated making his bed, but his bed is made. I'm glad I changed back into shorts and a T-shirt, because now I know that the heaviness in my stomach is plain sadness, instead of whatever had coiled up there beneath the dress.

I'm not really sure what I'm looking for. I start with his nightstand, opening the drawers. Not much in there— some foil packets, tissues, scattered medicine bottles.

I open his closet. His shirts are hanging up, like always, organized by color into a rainbow. I bet they still smell like him. I don't want to find out, so I close the door hastily. Whatever I'm looking for might be in there, but I'm still not ready to surround myself with what's left of him.

A gust of cold air brushes past me, but there's nowhere it could be coming from. I whip around and see the bed skirt swaying in the impossible breeze. Couldn't be a clearer hint. I get down on my belly, pull up the bed skirt, and immediately sneeze from the dust that puffs up around me. It settles around the clear plastic storage boxes lurking under his bed. I pull them out, one by one. It's hard to believe that there could be deep dark secrets about Uncle Roderick's life concealed in such plain, boring containers, but maybe that makes them the best hiding places.

I pull the lid off the first one, and it's full of random costume pieces. Lots of necklaces and bracelets and earrings. Some of them are pretty ugly and are probably jokes. Clunky huge plastic and wood, bright colors and gaudy tassels and rhinestones. Some of them might be nice, but I don't know much about jewelry, so maybe all of it is actually terrible. Or maybe all of it is beautiful. There are a few wigs scrunched up in a corner, random scraps of fabric. The next one is full of his makeup collection, painstakingly gathered over the years, still looking bright and brand-new.

A sudden flash of memory hits me. We're in his bedroom, sitting on the floor. I'm five years old, or somewhere around there, and we're playing dress-up. I remember draping necklace after necklace on him, and he's wearing a ridiculous tiara. I'm wearing one of his hats, a top hat, a tall and fancy thing made for a man from a hundred years ago. I tell him he looks beautiful. He tells me I look handsome. And I remember a glow deep inside my chest, like he was right, like he saw who I was going to be.

I jerk my head again, this time to shake out the memory. Someday I'll be ready to remember Uncle Roderick, but not today. Today I have to focus on what he's doing right now, and what I need to do. And I don't think this box is what he's guiding me toward.

I open the next box. This one is full of papers. One stack is all medical forms, and I flip through them quickly, avoiding any specific information about his diagnosis, treatment, prognosis. Another looks like random documents, *IRS* stamped in the corner, so probably tax stuff.

But most of the papers are something else. There's a

big folder with the letters *PFLAG* blazing across the front. Written in curly type underneath are the words "Parents, Family, and Friends of Lesbians and Gays."

I've heard about PFLAG before. It's a support group, I think? But Uncle Roderick never needed any support. He had us. I flip open the folder.

The first piece of paper is bright yellow, with the words "Transgender 101" written across the top. The one beneath it is green, titled "Local Resources for LGBTQ Youth." The one underneath is called "Our Stories," and it's a few pages stapled together. I skim through it, and it looks like stories of gay and lesbian and trans teenagers talking about themselves.

The rest of the box is filled with papers like this. Lots of newspaper and magazine articles, some about gay and lesbian people, but mostly about transgender people. There's an entire *Time* magazine, with an actress named Laverne Cox on the cover. And an issue of *National Geographic* with another trans person, this one a kid, on the front. There are some brochures and flyers and even some books jammed in there.

I know what "transgender" means. It means that someone is born one way, a girl or a boy, but that doesn't feel right to them, so they change. Maybe they take medicine or get different surgeries. I don't remember learning about it specifically, but Mom and Uncle Roderick would talk about it sometimes. I know they both had trans friends when they lived in the city, and sometimes those friends would visit. I remember being surprised when I found out that most kids lived with their mom and dad, because I hadn't figured out that having a father was normal. But people being LGBTQ was something I always knew about.

The only sound in the room is the rustle of papers and the rush of my breath. Then the floor creaks loudly behind me and I almost jump out of my skin. I whip around, almost expecting the ghost of Uncle Roderick to be drifting toward me (but then why would the floor creak? I don't know, nothing makes sense anymore), but it's only my mom.

"I called you a few times," she says, smiling sadly. So many of her smiles have been sad lately. I glance out the window, and the sun is shining through the trees. I hadn't realized how late it was.

"Sorry, I was distracted." It must be normal to go into someone's room after they die, to try and get a little bit of them back. I bet it's even in that book about death and dying. Mom doesn't ask why I'm doing it, probably because she did the same thing herself. It must be part of "acceptance," and I realize how lucky I am that this investigation looks like a normal stage of healing after someone dies. It keeps me from having to explain anything.

Mom settles on the floor next to me. "Where were you?" I ask.

She pulls up her knees, hugs them to her chest. "In town.

Looking around to see if there are any part-time jobs. No bites yet. I'm considering some other options." Those other options, a faraway city, turning our home into something else, hover above our heads like another kind of specter. "What were you looking at?" she asks.

I'm glad she's changing the subject. "I found these papers," I tell her. "Just wondering where they all came from."

She picks up a few, flips through them. "I mean, I know where the magazines and books came from," I explain. "But all the brochures and stuff? They're about, like, LGBTQ people. But I don't know where he could have picked them up."

"I recognize a lot of these," she says. "Some of them are old keepsakes from groups he was involved with in the city. And he liked to pick up information whenever we were somewhere with an LGBTQ center. Not because he needed it, I think, just because he liked the physical materials. Like a little archive, or museum."

I feel a sharp pain rise in my chest. I never knew these were here. I wish he had shared them with me. I don't want to look through them with Mom, but I don't know why. She knows that Uncle Roderick was gay, of course. She knows more about his life than I ever will. But this still feels like something between him and me. He wanted *me* to find these. There's something here he wants me to understand.

I put everything back in the bin, try to put them in

orderly stacks. Mom adds the few she picked up to the pile, and I shove the bin back under the bed.

My uncle isn't resting in peace, and these papers are related, somehow. I just know it.

fourteen

I'm back on Griffin's porch, book in hand. I looked through it for hours last night after dinner, but didn't learn anything more helpful about how to communicate with Uncle Roderick, or how much longer I had before he went to . . . wherever it is people go after they die.

"Hi again!" I say when he opens the door. "Sorry I didn't call first, I got caught in the rain yesterday and your number was in the pocket of my shorts. It got all smeared so I couldn't read it. But here, I brought your book back, good as new!"

I offer it to him, and he takes it. "I wouldn't say good as new," he says, and for a second I'm nervous. Does he think I damaged the book? But then he continues. "It's obviously like thirty years old. And has been checked out a bunch. So it's good as . . . old and very used. The librarian won't break my kneecaps for dog-earing a page, will she?"

I laugh, relieved. "When I was little my uncle had to return a book that I covered in mustard, and she didn't take away my library card. Or break my knees! I think you're fine."

"Phew." He hesitates for a minute. "Yesterday you were in a hurry," he finally says. "Do you have time to hang out? We could look for ghosts. Or just chill. But do you want to come in for a little bit, at least for some water? It's hot today."

It *is* hot today. And some cold water would be good. But yesterday the idea of coming inside sent me into a panic. I scan my body for stomach-dragonflies, dizziness, something telling me to stay away. There's nothing. I'm in basically the same outfit I was wearing the day we met at the library, worn jean shorts and a faded black T-shirt, but I feel less grubby than I did that day. And it's nothing like yesterday's dress.

"Sure!" I exclaim. "I'm pretty good at sensing ghosts and things. Let's explore."

We get some water and set off, knocking on walls, looking for hidden passageways, walking through rooms in a pattern, searching for cold spots. We stop talking every time we hear a creak.

It's fun. And easy. It feels like hanging out with Moira in that window in between when we hated each other and . . . whatever we are now. Whatever we're both growing into. I don't have a lot of experience with friendships, but maybe all this is normal. It would be nice to be normal at something.

It helps that looking for ghosts is something I'm *very* good at. Griffin sounds disappointed when I tell him that I've never seen a "real" ghost, like a translucent person floating above the ground and moaning. But he's very excited to find out that the cold spot in his kitchen is definitely from something supernatural. And that I sense some hovering presences in his basement.

"Are you *sure* you're just a human being?" he asks at some point, and I freeze for a second. Does he mean that I seem too weird to be human? But he continues with, "Like, you're not a ghostbuster, or psychic, or halfway between the human world and the spirit world? No one else ever seems to notice this kind of thing, but I can tell you're not making it up." I roll my eyes back into my head, pretend to go into a trance, and he starts yelling that whatever spirits have possessed my body should leave forthwith, and our laughter rings off the damp walls under his old house.

"How do you know about all this? It's more than just those library books, right?" he asks. We've quit our search and have moved to his porch with glasses of lemonade sweating in our hands.

"My uncle," I start. Knowing that I haven't said anything about him. That I'll have to explain. And of course Griffin is looking at me like he wants to know more.

"My mom's brother," I say. "He lived with us since I was a baby. He always told me about the different spirits and presences in our house. Not that he knew anything about them, like who they were or why they were there. But he was the one who told me about the cold spots, and that skin-prickling feeling, how that means there's one around. Our house is full of them."

I can tell he's about to ask another question, so I answer it. "He died. Uncle Roderick. At the beginning of the summer. He was sick."

"That sucks," says Griffin. "I'm so sorry."

"Thanks."

We drink our lemonade quietly for a minute. Then Griffin puts down his glass and stretches his arms above his head, and his T-shirt rides up just a bit. For a second I can see an expanse of skin above his shorts line. It's smooth and flat with a tiny bit of fuzz around his belly button, and suddenly I'm so, so jealous, but I don't know of what. We're about the same size, I've never really felt like I had to lose or gain weight, but suddenly I want to wear shorts and a T-shirt and have it look like that. Not like they do on me. Similar, but unnameably different. My stomach flips itself over again, like it did yesterday, and I don't want to ruin what a nice day we had by leaving in a weird, anxious, uncomfortable rush.

Luckily, it's about time I head home anyway. We finish our lemonade, dissecting the different kinds of spirits we might have sensed, which ones we think they are—actual presences, bursts of energy, or just memories held by a space. We talk about hanging out again, maybe me showing him around my house, and I get on my bike and point it toward home.

It was a relief to be around unfamiliar ghosts that weren't trying to tell me something. That weren't remnants of someone I love. As my bike careens down the dirt roads my mind is pulled back to the box under Uncle Roderick's bed.

I had read some of the stories in there, in different pamphlets and things, and they weren't what I had expected. For some reason I thought that being trans was all about your . . . you know, private parts. Like, knowing that they're wrong, and that you should have the other kind. But that almost never came up. A lot of the trans people telling their stories talked more about a general feeling of not-rightness. Like people looking at you through a frosted glass window, guessing at what they were seeing.

But that just sounds normal to me. It must be more of a human thing. I'm not trans, but I always feel like people are looking at me and seeing something wrong. Everything that's wrong with me, I mean. Even though none of it is anything that can be easily described. I look okay on the outside, but every piece of me just adds up to something not quite right.

And sure, that *could* mean that I'm trans too, but I know that it doesn't. Another thing all those articles were clear on is that trans people really are the genders they identify with. That arguments saying otherwise are transphobic, pure and simple. Like, a phrase I kept seeing repeated over and over again was "trans men are men" and "trans women are women." A sure, unshakeable truth. But I don't think that I *am* a boy. I don't feel like a boy that everyone thinks is a girl. I just feel like an uncomfortable, misshapen, squishy humanoid, and sure, *maybe* if I got to look like a boy and everyone thought I was a boy, that would make me feel better. Like if I looked more like Griffin, if my clothes fit like his did, if people looked at us and saw two boys together, I mean, of course I'd like that. But trans people *are* their genders. I just . . . *want*. Something. Which is different.

I wonder what it must be like to know something like that about yourself, know it clearly and truly, but not be able to live it, and then my legs go limp and rubbery and I almost fall off my bike at the side of the road. Suddenly, I'm sitting on the dirt crying, because the truth hits me all at once and it's so, so awful.

Uncle Roderick was transgender. I'm sure of it. That's what he wanted me to know. About being yourself. How he wasn't. Couldn't be. Why else would he have gathered all that information? Why else would he keep it under his bed? He knew, and he never told us.

Maybe he had a whole different name we should have been using this whole time. Maybe he—she? Maybe this was something that . . . they? Had wanted to do before dying. Oh no. With "Roderick" written on all those condolence cards. And all of our memories. Is this it?

Did this death come without anyone really knowing what was inside the person we all loved so much? I can't imagine anything worse, and it makes me want to break apart.

I hold my head in my hands and claw at my scalp, trying to make this somehow not true. Should I tell Mom? Or would that just make it worse? Two people realizing how we failed, instead of just one? But no. I have to tell her. She has to know. Maybe that's the only way for—for her sibling to rest in peace.

My legs are too weak for me to ride right now. I force myself off the ground, pick up my bike, and slowly walk home. I'm imagining what it would be like to have an aunt instead of an uncle. What she would have been like. The same, but different. What she would have needed from us, how fiercely we would have had to defend her. Or maybe it would have all been fine. Maybe the whole town would have been on her side, and our life would look exactly the same.

Something about these daydreams doesn't feel right, though. It's not hard to imagine the person my uncle was in a dress; he got dressed up sometimes and I loved to watch. He looked wonderful. But I can't imagine that person as . . . as a different person. Does that make me transphobic? Maybe that's why he—she—that's why we never knew this. That's why we were never told. Because maybe we wouldn't have been able to handle it.

But no. I would have. Maybe I would have taken some time to get used to it. But we all loved each other, and there's nothing that you can't do if you love someone.

It's not hard to walk my bike, but by the time I finally get home I'm panting, gasping for air, and my heart is pounding like a racehorse in my chest. The front door creaks open as I approach it and I feel a burst of wind at my back, propelling me toward Mom's studio.

She's at her desk, and looks up from the papers. It must be obvious that I'm not okay, because she drops them, comes over, and envelops me in a tight hug.

"Do you think Uncle Roderick was transgender?" I blurt out, my fists clenched against her back. I won't break down, I won't start to cry again. I hate the way tear stains look on the shoulder of her shirt, so I force myself to take some gulping deep breaths, shuddering a little, and slowly I get myself back under control. I pull out of her arms, and my breathing slows a bit.

"Sweetheart! What are you talking about? Are you okay?" Mom asks, and she sounds the kind of worried I never want her to be, like there's something wrong with me that she can't fix.

"That box I found," I gasp. "Remember? With all those pamphlets and books and everything. Some of them were just about being gay but a *lot* were about being trans. Is that what those were for?" I fling my hand up, like I'm pointing to the bedroom, the bed, the secrets hidden underneath. "All that information. Was he waiting for the right time to tell us?"

I pull back so I can look at Mom's face. She looks calm, maybe a little worried. "I don't think so . . ." she says slowly.

Does she sound uncertain? Or is she just trying to calm me down? "He would have told us, right?"

"Maybe? But I read some. A lot of these are stories from trans people about how their families didn't accept them. Maybe he was afraid"—my breath hitches, I almost lose it again—"that we would be like that."

Mom shakes her head. She looked so much like her brother, sometimes people mistook them for twins. I've never seen my face in hers, she says I take after my dad, but she and Uncle Roderick have the same eyes, the same cheeks. Had he wished that he looked more like her?

"Roddy knew himself," she says. "That was something I always admired about him. He was always so comfortable in his own skin no matter what anyone else thought. Do you remember that Halloween parade, where you two went as Beauty and the Beast?"

I was seven, and that Halloween sticks out. I had gone as the Beast. He had dressed up as Belle, in that yellow gown. "But couldn't that mean that maybe he wanted to wear dresses all the time?" I ask. "That he wanted to be a girl every day, not only one day a year?" Isn't it obvious?

Mom laughs. I can't remember the last time she laughed. "Definitely not, honey. I know he missed his drag queen days, so Halloween was the perfect time to pull out his old tricks. But do you remember what that woman from the grocery store said?"

The old woman who works the one cash register has been

there since before we moved here. She never says much to us. "I don't remember. What did she say?"

"She looked at you in your cute fuzzy Beast costume, and your uncle with his perfect hair and flowing gown, and said 'Isn't she supposed to be the Beauty, and you're supposed to be the Beast?'"

I had probably been too hopped up on candy to pay attention. "What did he tell her?"

"He said, 'We are both exactly who we are meant to be.' Roddy knew himself, and loved himself, and he wanted the same for you."

Mom hugs me again, and we just stand like that, for a while. I try to stop my brain from churning through all these possibilities and just feel my feet on the floor, her arms around me. The smell of laundry detergent on her shirt. After just the right amount of time she asks if I want dinner, so we go into the kitchen.

I chop cucumber for a salad. Mom grates carrots. I'm still turning over my sudden revelation, the new holes poked in it. The difference between wanting to be something, and knowing that you are something. How I can't quite picture what my aunt would look like, what that says about me.

I wonder if my mom is thinking about the same things. What her process would have been. And I have to know. "Mom?" I ask. "What would you have said, though? If he came out to you as trans."

She doesn't even pause to come up with an answer. "I would have had the most beautiful sister in the world. And I would have made sure that she got everything she needed to be herself."

I nod, but I'm still not sure. He kept those papers for a reason. And never told us about them, for some other reason. Dinner is a quiet occasion, and I don't think there are going to be any more answers here. Except for one.

My uncle knew he was loved. I still have a lot of questions, but that's not something I have to worry about.

fifteen

For the next two weeks I only sense the normal ghosts. Cold spots that feel nice in the early August heat. Empty rooms that have their own moods, their own memories. The mirrors are still playing their old tricks, but those are easy to avoid.

Mom believes that if Uncle Roderick was trans, he would have told us. And I want to believe her. But also, I haven't felt poltered since that day. I still have weird dreams, but they're normal-weird, just wisps of memory that vanish a few minutes after waking up. And no more strange objects have made their way into my room.

Maybe we won't be hearing from Uncle Roderick again. Maybe he—or she—is at rest.

Also, today is my twelfth birthday. Should I say something like "It sucks having a summer birthday" because kids who have school-year birthdays get to bring in cupcakes or doughnuts or whatever and everyone sings the happy birthday song at them? But I hate the happy birthday song, and I hate having a whole room full of people look at me.

My birthday parties have always been small—sometimes just Mom and Uncle Roderick, sometimes Moira or a few random kids from school. A homemade cake with candles flickering against the gathered faces, the sound of crickets playing outside. I love having a summer birthday.

I'm on my bike, heading to Moira's, backpack stuffed with an extra pair of underwear and socks and my pajamas. She called me yesterday, her voice sounding all innocent, asking what my plans were for dinner, if I wanted to come over to eat, and sleep over after. I pretended to believe she didn't remember it was my birthday, and told her I didn't have anything planned. She and her parents probably talked to Mom and have a cake ready. I wonder if this is my last birthday with her, and who I'll be at my next one.

I coast into their yard and hop off my bike. I open the front door and the foyer is dark. "Hello?" I call. "It's Bug!" And then the lights flick on.

My little scream of shock is drowned out by the loud refrain of "Happy birthday to you, happy birthday to you, happy birthday dear Bu-ug, happy birthday to you."

It's a surprise party? For me! I thought surprise parties only happen in books! But there's Moira, her mom and dad standing in the background, and a group of girls—Isla and Emily, and some I don't know. Balloons bob against the ceiling and there's a cake with thirteen candles, twelve red ones and a green one to grow on, set in the middle of their table.

I'm frozen in shock, and Moira bounds over and flings her arms around me.

"Happy birthday!" she squeals. I hug her back clumsily, my arms suddenly too long and too heavy to squeeze right.

"Thank you," I manage. My wide eyes are scanning the room over her shoulder. There are three girls I don't know, all of them dressed like Moira in bright sundresses or light-colored shorts and pretty T-shirts. Maybe they're called blouses. I should have worn that dress Moira gave me, instead of exactly what I'm always wearing. Part of me wishes I had known. I don't like surprises. Still, knowing that so many people went through all this trouble, for me . . . I almost start to cry, but swallow it back. Everyone cheers for me to blow out the candles and I do it in one puff, despite the tightness in my throat.

"Let me introduce you!" Moira gushes as the smell of candle smoke spreads throughout the room. "This is Hypatia, Chloe, and Chelsey." She points at each in turn, and I try to remember which is which. They're a little hard to tell apart. "I was at the mall getting new school clothes, and met them in the food court. They all started at Maplewood Middle School last year, so I thought I'd invite them! We can make new friends before we even start."

I'm a little embarrassed for her. Even I know that this isn't how you make friends, especially friends with cool older girls. But to my surprise, they're all smiling too. They come over and wish me a happy birthday, ask me how old I am, if I'm excited to start middle school, how long Moira and I have been friends. I can tell that Moira wishes I was going by my name, instead of Bug, but they don't comment at all. I guess if your name is Hypatia, "Bug" doesn't sound all that different.

We take the cake and head to the backyard, where Ellen has the grill all set up for a barbecue. There's a little dog back there, and as soon as we come out it starts zooming around me in circles, yapping maniacally.

"Brutus! Calm down!" shouts Chloe. It must be her dog. She tries to calm him, but he won't stop running and barking. He doesn't pay attention to anyone else, all his manic energy is focused on me. She grabs him by the collar and drags him away. "That's so strange," I hear her say as she clips on his leash and ties him to the porch. "He usually only barks at boys." Ellen throws Brutus a scrap of meat, and he settles down. And we just hang out.

It's different from that time Moira invited me to hang out with just Emily and Isla and those girls we already knew from school. These older girls don't seem to believe that we have to wear makeup or the right clothes to fit in. They bring up a couple boys, a couple times, but don't act like Boys is the most important conversation topic. They do tell us all about middle school. Not in a "we're smarter than you" way. More thoughtful than that, more useful. Which teachers to watch out for, how much homework to expect. It's not cliquish, they say, not a lot of drama to avoid, and we don't have to worry about bullies or anything. That sounds nice. I should have known that books about middle school are way more dramatic than real life.

As we all sit around the table with the chicken sausages that Ellen grilled, I have a sudden glimpse of what we look like from the outside. Like I'm hovering above the table, looking down. Six girls, with styled hair, some with bodies that are more, uh, developed than others, in clothes from the right stores in the mall. Talking and smiling like they all know some secret. And one person in grubby clothes, hair that isn't anything, sitting right in the middle like an ink splotch.

It gives me that same creeping sensation I get at home when I accidentally glance into a mirror and the face looking back isn't mine. I suddenly wonder if this is what it's like being a ghost—looking at the world from above, apart from it but wishing you were a part of it. Maybe ghosts haunt people because they want company.

If this scene happened in a book, the older girls would be a little mean to me. Not outright bullying, but subtly making sure I know that I'm not one of them. Emily and Isla would join in, because we were never really friends. And if this were in that same book, Moira would start acting like them, finally shedding her old friend like a peeling sunburn, and I would be sad and confused.

But that doesn't happen, and I'm slowly pulled into the group. When I ask a question, they listen. One or two of them answer. Emily wants to know about the different sports clubs, and Isla asks if there's a school newspaper. I don't talk much at first, because I haven't done anything this summer except be haunted by the ghost of my dead uncle/maybe trans aunt, and that's not the first impression I want to make. But the girls work at drawing me into conversation, and soon we're talking about our favorite subjects in school, bad cafeteria food, and whether it's better to do your homework first thing on Friday or save it till Sunday before bed. Moira sits next to me, sometimes leaning her body into mine a little, and I press back into her. I can't be the easiest person to stay friends with. Especially right now. But she's trying, and that means more than anything.

The sun sets and the mosquitoes come out in full force. Chloe has to go home, taking Brutus with her. I try to pet him farewell but he barks at me again. "So weird," says Chloe, shaking her head. "He's usually fine in big groups of girls. Anyway, happy birthday, Bug! Moira can give you my number, maybe we can hang out before school starts." Everyone says goodbye, and the rest of us troop inside.

When it's just Moira and me our sleepovers take place in her bedroom, with some excursions to the kitchen for snacks. But there are so many of us tonight that we go down into the basement. We settle down on the rug, and Hypatia tugs open her overnight bag and dumps the contents onto the floor.

I should have guessed. Nail polish, hair brushes and clips, lip gloss, other makeup things. Guess I do have to get used to this.

Chelsey asks if she can give me a makeover. I want to say no. They've all been so friendly, and I don't think anyone would be mean about it. But I say yes, because I want this to be something I understand. Something that I can do on my own. And, like the last time Moira gave me a makeover, it's mostly nice. Soft, light fingers, gently puffing breath, that feeling in my stomach of something twisting around, like a dog turning over and over before settling down to sleep. And this time, when I open my eyes and see myself in the mirror, I don't scream. I must be getting used to looking at a girl in the mirror. She's not bad.

Chelsey combs my hair, telling me how jealous she is. "I wish my hair wasn't so thin. Yours is super thick! I'm jealous."

"Thanks," I say. I never think about what my hair looks like. Sometimes I fantasize about shaving my head completely bald, palming the back of my head and rubbing my fingers against sharp stubble. I don't know why the thought is so comforting, but it is. Maybe someday I'll do it. Girls can have shaved heads too. But I don't think I'm that kind of girl. I'll figure out what kind of girl I am eventually. I have to, right?

We settle down for bed not long after midnight, our sleeping bags arranged in a circle. The cabinet under the bathroom sink is crammed full of grooming materials, and Moira pulls out a package of official makeup remover. Apparently you're not supposed to use soap and water. "Good thing we're not having this at Bug's house," Moira says through a yawn. "It's haunted."

"Is it really?" asks Hypatia.

"A little," I say. "But nothing's ever hurt me."

"Have you ever seen a ghost?" Chelsey wants to know.

I hesitate. "No," I say, and it's not a lie. "I've never seen one. But they're around. It's not a big deal."

"That's cool," says Emily. We chat a little bit more, my words coming easier in the dark. I'm not sure who falls asleep first, but in that space between awake and not, where everything is dreamy and warm and still, I imagine that the circle is a protection, that I'm safe with these girls. That I belong, somehow. And then I'm asleep.

sixteen

*A*nita Life has arrived, and she looks fabulous. Thick, curly silver hair cascading down her shoulders, dramatic makeup, long eyelashes framing her warm eyes. Her gown is made entirely out of dragonflies, green and blue and gold. They're still alive, flapping lazily and chirping like crickets.

We're walking somewhere. To a salon, cold tile floors and a warmly lit mirror. "You're going to look wonderful, darling," she tells me. She opens up her sequin suitcase and it's huge on the inside, stuffed with makeup and combs and wigs, with pipes snaking around like it's connected to a sink. She rummages through it, pulls out a set of electric clippers.

There's no barber chair. "You need to enter your life on your own terms," she tells me. "Are you ready?"

I pull my hair out of its ponytail and shake it down. It tumbles like ivy clinging to a building, moss trailing off a tree branch, cobwebs sticking to my face and neck.

"I'm ready."

seventeen

The smell of eggs and sausage and toast pulls me out of my dream. What was it? Snippets surface through my half-asleep haze. Uncle Roderick, in drag, in a barbershop? Weird. I've never been to a barbershop in my life. It's clear in my mind, like the creepy dreams from earlier in the summer, but more comforting. I half wonder if it's my last birthday present from Uncle Roderick. Like he—or she—is finally at peace, but gathered enough energy to give me this one last gift. Remembering Anita Life is a nice start to my thirteenth year.

I'm burrowed in my sleeping bag, surrounded by groggy girls stretching and yawning. "Good morning," whispers Moira, and scurries into the bathroom. I say it too, and the others join in. I sit up, rubbing my face with my hands, and try to pull back my hair. As my foggy brain slowly pieces together what my hands are telling me, I hear Moira scream, then I'm up and running.

She's in the bathroom, staring wide-eyed at the floor, which is covered in long, dark, snakelike shapes wildly strewn about. Her hands are clapped over her mouth. I'm running my hands over and over my head. Not through my hair. Over my head. The stubble that's left. A few lingering strands drop from my shoulders and slither down my neck onto the floor, where they join the deep pile carpeting the tile.

My hair is gone.

I shake my head, half wondering if this is a dream. There's an electric clipper, black and greasy, sitting on the sink, still plugged into the wall. The blade is clogged with dark hairs. I pick it up and turn it over in my hands. It's heavy.

The others crowd into the bathroom, their voices a jumble. "What happened?" "Your HAIR!" "HOW did that—" "Did you—" "I *thought* I heard—"

All I know is, he's here. Uncle Roderick. He followed me. He did this.

There's no other explanation. I don't believe that any of my new friends would do something like this. That would be mean, and they're not mean.

The dream, I remember with a start. Anita Life. The salon. *"Enter your life on your own terms,"* she told me. *"I'm ready,"* I said. Did we do this . . . together? I pet my head, over and over, with shaking hands.

"Did you . . . did you do this last night?" asks Moira uncertainly.

"No," I say, still staring at the floor.

"I mean, maybe not on purpose. Do you think you sleep-walked? Sleep-barbered?"

I shake my now-lightened head. "You know I've never sleepwalked in my life. I didn't even know these clippers were here. There's no way I did this." Too late I realize that if I'd lied, told them I wanted to try out a new look, some birthday impulse, that might have been okay. Quirky, and fun. But it's too late for that.

"You know," says Hypatia thoughtfully, "this is extremely creepy. But . . . you look good?"

I hadn't thought about what I look like. I'm avoiding the mirror, out of habit. "I do?" The words come out quavering.

"Yeah," says Isla. "I mean, I'm freaked the heck out. Especially since the last thing we talked about was how you live in a haunted house. But it works for you. Maybe a ghost came over and did you a favor?"

She's joking, but she might be right. Moira's eyes are wide, her mouth still open, but there's a look on her face that says she doesn't believe it's a joke. Uncle Roderick didn't want to talk to her through the Ouija board, but maybe he was watching us. I look at Moira, my eyes asking her something. I'm not sure what, but I'm asking.

She closes her mouth, blinks a few times. "Yeah," she says. Her voice sounds a little tight, but if you didn't know her well you might not notice it. "I like it."

"Can you . . . can you all give me a minute?" I ask. They nod. Chelsey pats my shoulder as she leaves. I close the door behind them, settling my gaze again on the pile of hair on the floor. I should clean it up. I dump handfuls into the garbage can. What if they're lying? What if I look terrible? But I pet my scalp again, it's bristly and soft. Comforting. Something I don't even need to get used to, I like it right away.

Still rubbing my head, that scratchy sensation calming me down, I straighten up. Drop my palm. And slowly look into my own eyes.

And it's me. Just me.

There he is, I think. Then I stop thinking, for just a second, and feel.

I see a boy in the mirror. I see myself in the mirror. Every other time I've looked in a mirror, I've seen a girl, and not seen myself. I've always thought it was a ghost. Or a trick. But there he is. There I am. And I realize.

This is what Uncle Roderick wanted me to know. *This* is what he was trying to tell me. This is why he was holding on to those papers under his bed. He was waiting for me to be ready. He knew.

Everything comes together, a whirl of understanding tearing through my mind like a hurricane. Breaking the nail polish bottle after I got that first makeover. Talking to me through the Ouija board "Be you" when I came home wearing that dress. I didn't like any of those things, I didn't want to do any of those things, and Uncle Roderick must have been trying to tell me that it was okay. That I didn't have to like them. That I didn't have to try to be a girl. All I had to do was be myself—a boy.

I don't know how long I'm in the bathroom, staring at myself, letting this new truth flicker inside me like a candle. Long enough for Moira to start banging on the door.

"Bug! What are you doing in there? Are you okay?"

"I'm okay," I call out. Even my voice sounds different, now that I know. Not deeper. But more real. More mine. I wonder if Moira can hear it.

I unlock the bathroom and come out slowly. I feel like I'm standing up, up, up. My shoulders pulled back. My neck, straight and strong. Every step turns into a stride. Moira's standing right outside the bathroom. She looks worried, but a smile slowly crosses her face like a rising sun.

"You do look good," she says. But something spreads underneath her words, something more.

"Thanks," I say. "I feel good." I'm sure she hears under my words too.

The other girls sense that something big has happened, even if they don't know what. They give me hugs that I don't instinctively recoil from, and tell me again that it suits me. "I know," I say, and we all laugh. Then we go upstairs for breakfast.

Moira's mom is surprised, of course. "Bug, your hair! What happened?"

"It looks so good, right?" asks Moira. I'm a little surprised she didn't say "She looks good," but not really. It's obvious.

"Yeah," Hypatia chimes in. "It works way better with her face shape and style and everything." Is it just me, or did I hear a pause before she called me "her"? It sounds wrong, all of a sudden. No. Not all of a sudden. It's always sounded wrong, but now I know why. I want to tell them to call me "he" now, but I should probably wait and talk to Mom first.

Speaking of. "Well, so long as your mom is okay with it, Bug," says Ellen.

"She will be," I say. "She always says I can do whatever I want to my hair. I've just never felt like it before."

"How did it happen?" asks Ellen. "Or do I not want to know?"

"You don't want to know," I say. To my surprise, all five of us say it at the exact same time. Then we start to laugh.

We help clean up after reducing breakfast to crumbs. "I should go," I say, loading my plate into the dishwasher. "Thank you so much for the surprise party! It was way more fun than I expected to have on my birthday."

"Of course," says Moira. She hugs me tight, and I hug her back. I'm a boy hugging a girl now, as friends, and it's the first time that hugging her doesn't make me feel awkward, or stiff, or gross. Just like a friend. I hug the other girls too, tell them I'm excited to see them in middle school, and I mean it.

Moira walks me out with my sleeping bag and backpack. "Let me know if you want to go to the mall with me sometime," she says. She sounds more serious than usual. "We can get you clothes that match your, um, haircut."

She's saying something else, and we both know it. "I'd like that," I tell her. "Just let me talk to my mom first."

She nods. "Bye, Bug. I'm glad we're friends."

"I am too," I say, and hop onto my bike.

eighteen

Racing along the rough and winding roads that lead to my house, I'm not nervous at all. I'm going to tell Mom that I'm a boy. She'll hug me and kiss my shorn head and tell me that she loves me no matter what. We'll buy me new clothes, I'll pick a new name, every part of myself that never fit before will snap into place.

My bicycle wheels crunch through gravel and dry dirt, but I feel like I'm soaring above it all. And yet I'm more *here,* more *present,* than I've ever been before. That first moment I saw myself in the mirror at Moira's house switched on a light bulb inside of me. Now I imagine taking a flashlight, rooting around in an attic, the bright beam illuminating dusty corners and the truths hiding in them.

But my excitement drains away the closer I get to home. Worry replaces it, drip by steady drip.

Mom said that she would have been fine if Uncle Roderick was trans. She sounded like she meant it. But does that mean that she'll be okay with me? I start to remember snatches of the stories I read from the box under Uncle Roderick's bed. *It felt like my daughter had died. My parents still call me by my old name. We fought every day for a year.* Only a few of the stories were about parents who got it right away. My legs turn the pedals slowly, then even more slowly until I can barely balance, wobbling down the driveway. But soon I roll up to the old house, the pointed eaves looking down at me. I half drop, half fall off my bike. Whatever will happen next, will happen. Mom has always been honest with me, and now it's my turn to finally be honest with her. To tell her the truth. I've only known what that truth is for a morning, but can't imagine waiting another second to start the rest of my life as myself.

I skip up the creaky steps. Our front door, usually so heavy, springs open at my touch like an eager puppy. I pet my head, loving the shape of my skull against my hand, and I can't imagine ever wanting a different haircut. Mom's in the kitchen, sitting at the table with a cup of coffee. She looks up and sees me, then does a double take and looks at me again. Emotions play across her face, too many and too fast for me to read, but they end in a smile, a smile that goes all the way up into her eyes.

First reveal done. I sit down across from her and try to breathe.

"Nice haircut," she says. "It was a fun sleepover?"

"Yeah," I say. I planned a bunch of different speeches on the bike ride home, some of them starting with "Remember the box we found under Uncle Roderick's bed?" or "You know how you said you would love your brother even if he was your sister?" But none of those scripts find their way out.

"Mom," I say. "I'm a boy."

Her coffee mug pauses in transit to her mouth, reverses back to the table. I watch it go, afraid to raise my eyes up to her face.

A moment passes. Then I hear her voice, and it's filled with love. "You're telling me that you're transgender?" she asks.

I nod. And lift my head. Sit up straight. Look into her eyes. "Yes. When I woke up this morning, when I saw myself in the mirror, I knew. I've never recognized myself before, but now I do. Are you—" My voice, so sure a second earlier, starts to tremble. "Is it—"

Mom gets up from her chair. Comes around the table. And puts her arms around me. "Yes," she says. And we both start to cry.

People cry at beginnings and at endings, and this moment is one of each. They're not sad tears. Or, at least, the sad tears are mixed in with the others, and are sneaking their way out. I'm crying for my uncle, and a little for myself. She is crying for her brother, maybe her husband, maybe her daughter and son, maybe other tears that she's never told me about.

Once we're both cried out, she takes my wet face in both hands and looks into my eyes, which are probably as red and puffy as hers. "My beautiful boy," she says. And I know, I just *know*, that Uncle Roderick is here, watching us, wishing he could be at the scarred old table in more than spirit.

I tell her everything. Starting with my suspicions about the broken nail polish bottle, the dramatically haunted night that led to the library trip, the Ouija board, that last dream and how I know that I didn't shave my head by myself.

"That sounds pretty scary," she says.

"Only a little! I mean, it's Uncle Roderick, right? I could never be scared of him."

Mom nods slowly. "That makes sense." But I hear what she's not saying.

"You don't believe me, do you?" I ask.

"Believe you? Oh honey, of course I believe you." She pauses, picking her words carefully. "We both miss Roddy very much. And when you're keeping a lot inside, it can come out in strange ways. Even if I'm not completely sure that the ghost of my brother came back to tell you about yourself, I still believe that you experienced some very strange things."

"If you had been there you would believe me." I guess I'm lucky. Mom believes that I'm trans. And she's never believed in ghosts. It could be worse.

She shrugs. "Maybe he did that on purpose. 'There are more things in heaven and earth, Horatio, than are dreamt of in your philosophy.'"

"Huh?"

"Shakespeare."

"Oh."

"Indeed. I'm the Horatio here. But don't worry, sweet prince, no flights of angels for you."

I have no idea what she's talking about. But she sounds like herself, and I'm happy about that.

nineteen

The next morning I wake up from a normal dream, fleeting shards of barely memory, and look around my room. Nothing has visited it in the night, nothing's different. But inside of me, everything is different.

I have to tell Moira. The way she reacted to my haircut is a good sign, she clearly understood that there was something bigger going on. I don't think she'll suddenly hate me, or think that I'm crazy, but after I call to invite her along on a mall trip I rehearse some answers to questions she might ask. The pamphlets under Uncle Roderick's bed come in handy.

She bikes over a couple hours later, and before we leave Mom gives us some space. I sit Moira down at the kitchen table with a glass of lemonade.

"Something's going on," she says. "You've never asked me to go shopping with you before. What is it? Are you moving? Redecorating your room?"

I grin. She has no idea. "I'm a boy," I tell her. Best to just barrel ahead, get it all out at once. "The word for that is 'transgender.' You can still call me Bug for now, but I'm going to choose a new name and might start going by that before the first day of school. Or I might wait till later, I'm not sure yet." No matter what her response is, just saying it makes me feel powerful. Awake. Like everything before this has been a dream that I'm just waking up from.

She chokes on her lemonade and starts coughing. I laugh. "Sorry, should have waited for you to swallow."

She swats at me, her face beet red. "You really should have!" she strangles out. "Way to practically kill your best friend." She takes another sip, and slowly her color returns to normal.

Whatever anxiety I felt subsides when she calls herself my best friend. "Do you have any questions?" I ask her seriously. "About what it means to be transgender, or anything? It's okay if you do."

She tosses her head confidently. "No, I'm good. I've seen some TV shows where it's a thing. And some magazine articles. I'm not an expert or anything, but it's not that confusing."

"Oh! Okay, cool." I'm a little surprised. I had thought she'd need more of an explanation, but I guess I underestimated her. "And . . . you're okay with it? You still want to be my friend? Do you need time to get used to it?"

She rolls her eyes. "I mean, it's not really something I get be 'okay with,' right? It's just, like, who you are. And honestly, this is probably going to make it so much easier to make friends! You make *such* a cute boy. We're going to have no trouble fitting in!"

A wave of anger rushes over me, obliterating any relief I had felt. How can someone start by doing such a good job and then completely ruin it? "Is that all you can think about?" I snap. "Fitting in? Making new friends? Well, I'm *so glad* that me coming out as transgender is going to help you sit with the popular crowd!"

"That's not what I mean, Bug," she says, sounding exasperated. "We both knew you were going to have a hard time making friends. Probably because you didn't know who you were! And now you do. You're different. More comfortable. It's obvious! I know you know I'm right, everything is going to be different for you now. In a good way. You won't just be stuck with me. That should make you happy, shouldn't it?"

"I think you mean *you* won't be stuck with *me* anymore." I clench my hand around my lemonade glass.

"Maybe both," she says, but she sounds less angry. Almost like she's said something she's been thinking for a long time, and it's a relief to get it out.

My jaw is gritted shut, but I try taking a few breaths. This wasn't supposed to turn into a fight. "Look," I say, as evenly as possible. "We should probably just figure this out now. We don't have to be friends anymore. It was never easy for us to get along anyway, and now we can just stop trying.

Even if I don't make a million new friends right away, that doesn't have to be your problem." I didn't think that me coming out as transgender would end our friendship, at least not like this. But maybe it's been slowly ending for months, and this is just the final stage. And being honest with others is part of being true to myself.

But Moira shakes her head. "I've never felt like you were my problem," she says softly.

"You sure treat me like one sometimes," I grumble. A little voice whispers that I've always *felt* like a problem, but I tell it to shush. "This whole summer has been you trying to get me to wear makeup, nail polish, do my hair. What was I before, if not something you were trying to fix?"

Moira looks like she's about to cry. "I'm *sorry!*" she says. "I was just trying to help! You should have told me that you hated that stuff. I didn't know."

The spike of anger hasn't receded completely, but a pang of guilt threads its way through. How could she know who I was if I didn't? "I didn't hate it, exactly," I say grudgingly. "It was just wrong. And I didn't know how to explain it. I guess I thought that if I convinced everyone else that I was good at being a girl, I would start to feel like one. Like if I fooled everyone else into believing that I was perfect, like you, that would be the same as actually feeling that way. Does that make sense?" I had expected to answer her questions about, like, transitioning, or pronouns. Not about how I've been feeling all summer, or forever. About me, and her, why we've always felt so different. It's hard to put into words, but now I feel like I owe it to her. And to myself.

Moira laughs through held-back tears. "Hang on. You think I'm *perfect*? Me? Do you know how many hours I've spent studying this stuff, colors and techniques and everything? I learned more from your uncle than anyone else, and now I don't know what I'm going to do. It's *hard*!"

"Really?" I say in disbelief. "But you always seemed to get it. It all came so naturally to you, all of a sudden you're like a teen model and I'm still some troll."

She shakes her head. "Nothing comes naturally to me, Bug. You're the one who gets good grades and corrects the teacher's spelling and is in the highest reading group. And honestly . . ." She looks down at the wet ring her glass left behind on the table, starts smearing it around with her index finger. "It felt nice to be better at something than you, for a change. You've never been afraid to be different. I've always been a little jealous of you for that."

I rub my palm against my shaved head. Moira, jealous of me? That doesn't even seem possible. But she has no reason to lie, so I guess it must be true. "Well, maybe all that work wasn't for nothing," I reassure her. "Boys can wear nail polish. And makeup. Maybe I'll want to be that kind of boy. Heck, maybe now we'll have *more* in common."

Moira lets out a shaky breath. She still won't look at me.

"Maybe. But I'm sorry for trying to turn you into someone you're not."

She's still playing with the ring of condensation. I poke her index finger with mine, and finally she meets my eyes. "You were trying to help," I admit, not letting her look away. "And you weren't wrong. I did want to figure out who I was by the time middle school started. It's just that we needed different things."

I wonder what our friendship would have looked like if I had been a boy all along. I mean, if everyone had known I was a boy. I think *that* was the friendship we were always meant to have, and I can tell Moira feels it too. I have a sudden flash of sympathy for her, being stuck hanging out with a mopey grump that never wanted to do anything she thought was fun, always acting like something was wrong no matter what she did. I'll make it up to her.

Moira nods, and rubs her eyes. Then she grins hugely. "Well? Why are we still hanging around this haunted old house? Let's go shopping!"

Mom drives us to the mall, and we chatter excitedly the whole way. And all of a sudden I understand why people like shopping. I mean, I don't *love* it. I'd still rather read, or ride my bike. But now that Moira is helping me pick from the boys' section instead of the girls', it's actually fun. We make a pile of different T-shirts in soft fabrics with interesting patterns and funny jokes. And jeans! I love boy jeans.

They have pockets. And they aren't so tight. I take an arm-load into the boys' fitting room and no one blinks an eye. I spend so much time admiring myself in the mirror that Moira starts to yell at me from outside.

"Come *on*! I wanna see what you look like! Let me help you pick outfits!"

So I run back and forth showing her different shirts and jeans. Like going-to-the-mall scenes in books or movies, which I'd always skip over because they seemed boring. This isn't boring. We take almost everything, including one dark pink shirt, and a purple one with yellow flowers. I mean, they're from the boys' section, right? I never wanted to wear pink or purple before, but it's different now that people won't look at me and see a girl in a pink shirt. Mom pays for everything, and I have a moment of panic—can we afford all this? But she seems relaxed about it, so I decide to trust her. We've already survived two huge changes, and we'll make it through anything else that comes our way.

twenty

I don't think I've ever been this excited to go to school. I'm jumping up on the porch, making the front door swing open and shut in a matching beat. It might just be responding to vibrations from the floorboards, but I think it's my haunted house telling me to get a move on, get started already. "Mom! Come *on*! We're going to be late!"

"Your school is forty-five minutes away. You have to be there at eight thirty. It is currently seven a.m., and I am not done with my coffee."

"Ugh. Fine. I'll go wait by the car."

"You do that." Mom sounds grumpy, but I can hear a smile in her voice. What mom doesn't want her kid begging to start the first day of school?

Last week Mom drove me to the school for a meeting with the principal. She had called a few different LGBT organizations for advice, and they suggested that she set up a meeting with the school administration, to make sure that I'd get any support I needed. I didn't know what to expect, so I was jittery as we sat outside Principal Campbell's office.

The building was hot and stuffy but smelled fresh somehow, like it was waiting to welcome us.

The door opened and Mrs. Campbell ushered us inside. Her warm smile contrasted with slightly concerned eyes.

"Good morning! You must be Sabrina. And this is?"

"This is my son, Bug," said Mom. Mrs. Campbell shook my hand like I was an adult, and we sat down.

"So what can I do for the two of you? My secretary says you wanted assurance that your son would have some particular needs met, is that right?"

"Yes, that's right. Bug has recently come out as transgender. We want to make sure that the school is prepared to treat him like a boy, despite what his records say. We also want to make sure that there is an anti-bullying policy, that he's permitted to use whichever restroom is most comfortable, and that his teachers will be asked to refer to him exclusively as 'Bug,' instead of his legal name, and with male pronouns."

I kept a close eye on Mrs. Campbell during Mom's little speech. We had agreed that she would start the conversation, so the principal would know for sure that she was on my side. I could answer questions and talk about what I wanted too, but we thought it was a good idea for Mom to introduce me.

The older woman's face didn't change at all. The same warm smile, the same concerned eyes. She looked back and forth between me and Mom, but I didn't get the sense that she was staring at me *or* avoiding me. When Mom finished and steepled her hands on the desk, Mrs. Campbell took a deep breath, and seemed to organize her thoughts before speaking.

"First, let me say thank you for being so proactive. I can tell that Bug has a strong network of support, and that is the key to success in middle school.

"Second, as far as I know, Bug will be our first transgender student. But the administration and teaching staff operate under the assumption that any child could be transgender, or identify in some other way that they haven't shared with us. Some of our restrooms are gender-segregated, but we have five single-stall restrooms evenly spaced throughout the building. Bug can use whichever ones he thinks are best. I'll make sure the name 'Bug' appears on the attendance charts, and in case his legal name is also on there, I'll let his teachers know to keep that confidential."

I stared at her, my mouth open. I had let myself hope that this meeting wouldn't be terrible, but was also prepared to fight. I didn't want to argue about how real and valid my identity was, but knew I might have to. I wasn't expecting her to be so ready. Nothing that I read had prepared me for this.

The pause hung in the air. I guessed it was my turn to say something. "Um, thank you, Mrs. Campbell. That all sounds very . . . good." *Great,* I thought, *way to show her you can speak for yourself.* I came up with something serious to ask. "My mom mentioned an anti-bullying policy, do you think that's something I'll have to worry about? You talked a lot about the teachers but not much about the kids." My birthday party with Chelsey and Chloe and Hypatia gave me a good first impression of this place, but I was still nervous about meeting hundreds of new people.

Mrs. Campbell nodded firmly. "We do have an anti-bullying policy, and all faculty and staff have been to trainings around that issue. We know what to look for, and we know how to intervene without escalating. Of course, middle school is a time when you and your classmates will be dealing with insecurities, friendships, relationships, puberty. It's not an easy time to be a person, and conflict and hurt feelings are a part of life. But if you think you're being targeted or harassed, you can bring those concerns directly to me, or any of your teachers, and we will take it seriously."

I nodded. I liked that she was talking to me like an adult. Well, not like an adult, but like a human being she respected.

"Do you have any other questions right now? Have you been to this school before? I'm happy to take you on a quick tour." Mom and I agreed, so Principal Campbell took us on a quick lap of the building—the science lab, the gym ("No locker rooms," she said, pointing to a long row of stalls against one of the walls), and all the bathrooms. By the time she said goodbye, I was grinning. "The boy couldn't wait to start school," I thought to myself for a second, but it didn't feel right. I couldn't wait, but it was just true, not something I had to tell myself.

So, yeah, I'm pretty excited to get to school today. It's funny, Moira spent all summer talking about how middle school would be a fresh start, and I didn't believe her. I couldn't have imagined that a new year could be a beginning in so many ways. I'm wearing one of my new outfits: neatly cuffed dark shorts (it's hot out still), a white polo shirt with little green frogs all over it, and a new pair of gray sneakers. Mom finally drags herself out of the house, a travel mug of coffee in hand, and I jump into the car.

"Hey Bug? I've been meaning to tell you," says Mom about halfway there, "or thank you, I guess. You saved our house."

"What?" I had been staring out the window, wondering if Uncle Roderick was really gone for good. Wondering if he was still hovering around enough to hear me talk to Moira, see me in my new outfits. I hope so. But Mom snaps me back to the here and now.

"I had started to look into selling, and moving us to an apartment close to your school. I've been telling you all summer that business is down, but didn't tell you . . . quite how down it was."

Normally this line of conversation would make me nervous, but there's an ease to her voice that I haven't heard for a long time. "After you came out," she continues, "I got an idea for a whole new line of cards. Snarky ones for gay weddings and gay divorces, updated birth announcements, gender reveal parties for adults, et cetera. I've spent the past week talking on the phone with all of Roddy's and my old friends to come up with ideas for a whole line of queer celebrations."

I'm staring at her now, my jaw dropped in delight. "For real? That's the best idea I've ever heard! We're going to be millionaires!"

Mom laughs. "Probably not, but I'm still very excited. I made some mock-ups, sent them out to a handful of our best retailers, and demand is through the roof. I know you've been worried for a while, but we're in the clear, for now at least."

We don't have to leave our house. Our garden. The creek where I heard Uncle Roderick's voice. I'm trembling, just slightly, this possible version of my tiny family's future brushing up against me like a sideswiping truck.

"That's great," I say. Mom can hear the shake in my voice and looks at me for second.

"What's wrong?" she asks.

I open my mouth to say "Nothing," but something spills out instead. Something I didn't even know had been building up. "I was so *worried*, Mom! Uncle Roderick died, and suddenly we don't have any money and have to sell the only home I've ever known and move somewhere else? I know you've always been honest with me, and I know you felt like you had to tell me, but—" My voice breaks. Mom has stopped the car, pulled over onto the shoulder. She's looking at me like she's about to cry too, and I'm glad we left with so much extra time.

"But it was too much."

I wipe my eyes. "Yeah. It was too much."

"I'm sorry, son," she says. Her hands are still on the steering wheel, and she's looking out the windshield. But I don't think her eyes are focused on anything. "You've always seemed so mature for your age. And if worst came to worst, and we did have to move, I didn't want it to come as a sudden surprise. I wanted you to have time to prepare. But I guess I forgot that my first job isn't to prepare you. It's to protect you, as best I can." She unbuckles her seat belt, reaches over, and hugs me tight.

I let out one shuddering breath. Release something I had been holding, and feel her take it, lightly.

"Thanks," I say, once my voice is under control. "You can repay me for the emotional distress in room and board and new clothes every school year. Deal?" I'm not sure if she's up for teasing just yet, but she grins and tells me it's a deal.

And just like that, we're at my new school. Mom pulls up behind the school buses, kisses my forehead. I shoulder my backpack and stare at the big brick building, kids streaming through the open front doors. I take a deep breath, and join them.

twenty-one

I had thought that this day, all by itself, would be something bigger for me. The first day of the rest of my life as a boy, as a transgender boy. I almost start to picture it like it would be in a book, a boy slinging his backpack over his shoulders, walking up the front steps, but it doesn't work. And I realize, I haven't really imagined myself from the outside since coming out as trans. It's right to think of myself as a boy, but wrong to picture it like it's happening to someone else. I want to experience this day and every day as myself. Me, the real me, not some other boy.

And now that it's begun, it doesn't feel like some big climax. It's just a first day of school. Teachers outline the work we'll be doing over the year. They all call me Bug, and nobody laughs or comments on my name. It's exciting, because everything is new, and also a little boring, because the first day of school is always a little boring. I see some kids I recognize from elementary school, kids who have known me my whole life, and we all say hi and how was your summer, and a few people tell me that they like my haircut but no one says much more than that.

I'm a little on edge, though. How do I tell people that I'm a boy now without it turning into something big? Moira and I have our first couple classes together; we talk about my options while walking from one to the other.

"How about at lunch?" she says. "All the seventh graders have lunch at the same time. I'll ask a bunch of kids from our old school to sit at the same table, like a mini-reunion. You can tell them then. Does that sound okay?"

"Yeah," I say. I wish there was another way, but short of inventing telepathy or memory control between now and lunch, this seems like the best approach. I cross my fingers and hope for the best.

In the cafeteria (which is also the gym and smells loudly of hot dogs underlain with basketballs) I find Moira, sitting in the middle of one of those long tables with benches attached, surrounded by six or seven kids I went to elementary school with. No one I knew very well. Isla and Olive are there too; they smile at me.

I sit down with my tray, and everyone says hi. The conversation keeps going like it did before I sat down, and I'm quiet for a bit, but I don't feel left outside of it. I'm there, considering my options.

Then I hear a voice behind me. "Excuse me, can I sit here?"

I turn around. "Griffin!" I cry.

"Hi Bug! Happy first day of school!"

"You too! You can totally sit with us." I scoot over to make room, and Griffin sets down his tray. I explain where we met, and he tells everyone about his move from Portland. I glance over at Moira, and she gives me a look that definitely means *He's so cute, how dare you not tell me about him.* I blush, a little, because he's definitely cute.

"Anyway," Griffin wraps up. "That's why I'm here. Nice haircut, by the way!" That's as good an opening as any, I guess.

"Thanks," I tell him. "I came out as transgender over the summer, and this haircut works better for me now." I don't mention the part about the ghost. Neither does Moira.

"Cool," says Griffin.

"Transgender?" asks a girl named Sophie. "Like that girl on YouTube? Jazz?"

"Yeah," I say. "I mean, I'm not exactly like her, because I'm a boy. But yeah."

"Like my cousin!" exclaims another girl, Polly. "He's transgender. Like you. The boy kind, I mean."

"You want us to call you 'he' and 'him' instead of 'she' and 'her,' right?" Moira asks. I know she knows the answer, but am grateful for the opportunity to tell everyone.

"Yes please. Also, um, could you guys not tell anyone? I don't know if I want other people to know yet."

"Totally," said this boy Jeremy. "I'm gay, and it's cool and everything, but I don't want people to know that until I want them to know that. Which might be as soon as I put a rainbow pin on my backpack? But not until then."

"Exactly!" I say, grinning. "I won't tell anyone that you're gay, either."

Jeremy holds his hand up for a high five, and I give it to him. For the rest of lunch we talk about middle school things. Classes and teachers and what we're worried about and what we're excited about. And I'm there with them, not hovering around or above, watching silently. Not a ghost, or a character in a book. Just there, as my whole self.

I've suddenly made a whole bunch of new friends, who just happen to be people I've known forever. But, in some ways, we've only just met each other.

I come home brimming with stories. I know I close the front door behind me when I bound across the threshold, but it swings itself open again. Like the whole house has its ears perked up, wanting to hear about my day. I gush about which teachers are going to be my favorites, all the different clubs I can join, lunch, the new friends I made. Mom rests her head on her fist, and as I go over every detail her eyes sparkle with tears.

"I'm so happy for you, kiddo," she says, but she doesn't look happy. She sees the question in my eyes. "I'm just think-ing about Roddy," she explains. "How thrilled he would be for you too. I wish he were still here."

This summer must have been harder for Mom than for me. We both spent it missing him. But I was allowed to mope around, wade in the creek, read books on the porch, and miss him with nothing else to do. She had to miss him and also plan his memorial. Try to keep a business afloat. Take care of me.

Plus, it's hard to miss someone when his ghost is hovering around. He had been communicating with me, but there was nothing Uncle Roderick wanted to tell her. And I've had the whole being trans thing to distract me. I wonder if I'll start missing him even more now.

"I have so many questions for him now," I tell her. "He wasn't much older than me when he came out as gay, right?"

"Sixteen."

"Do you know how he did it? Did he tell everyone right away? Or did he tell you guys first, and then his friends?"

"I remember it being the other way around," she says. "He started telling his best friends first. He told me next, and asked how I thought our parents would handle it. I told him that I wasn't surprised, and they probably wouldn't be, either. They weren't. But I'll never forget how tightly he squeezed my hand at dinner that night, as he was telling them. He was so afraid they were going to yell, or curse, or throw him out, all of the terrible things he had heard about happening to other gay kids. But Mom hugged him. Our stepfather went over to the fridge and pulled out a bottle of sparkling cider, which we usually saved for special occasions, and poured us all a glass. And from then on it was a non-issue."

"I wish I could talk to him about it," I admit. "The kids I

had lunch with know, but I don't know how to tell new people. Or if I want to. I'm not sure if I want the whole school to know I'm transgender, or if I want to keep it mostly private."

"And if some people know, there's no way to keep anyone else from finding out."

"Yeah," I say. Like when a kid in a different class had open-heart surgery. He never told me, but everyone knew anyway.

"Are you worried that the kids from your old school will talk about it?"

"Mmm . . . not really. I think they all got why that wouldn't be cool."

"Well, you don't have to know all the answers right away. For now, at least, it seems private enough. Why don't you spend some more time thinking it over? Talk to Moira, or your other friends. I'm still looking for a support group for you that isn't hours and hours away. We'll read books together. Ultimately it's your decision, but I want you to have as much information as possible before deciding what path to take."

She's right. If I were one of the kids I read about in books—not only books about trans kids but all kinds of books about kids with something going on in their lives— I'd do something big, and rash. Maybe I'd make a big speech at an assembly about my journey that would leave everyone crying, and I'd win some award at the end of the school year that I definitely didn't deserve. Or I'd decide to be as normal a boy as possible and join a sports team and then a bad thing would happen to me in the locker room. I'd tell everyone that I have a birth defect or something, and spend the rest of my life hoping that no one found out the truth. That all sounds like a lot of effort.

Instead, I unwind after the first day of middle school. I do the little bit of homework, a math assessment and notes on the first chapter of our history textbook. I read about the different student organizations I could join, and check out the instructions for how to start a new one—there's no LGBTQ group yet, but there could be.

Mom says she wants to turn in early. She pours herself a glass of wine, and pads up the stairs. I'm still on the couch when I hear her gasp, loudly. "You okay?" I call.

"Bug, could you come here for a minute, please?" There's a barely disguised panic behind her words.

I bound up, past Uncle Roderick's still-closed door. Mom's standing next to her bed, something dangling from her hand that glints in the light.

"Sweetie, did you put this here?" Her voice is shaky.

"No, what is it?" I get a closer look and realize it's a heart locket on a gold chain. I've never seen it before.

"This was . . . this was something Roddy gave to me. After your father died." She clicks it open and carefully places it in my palm. There's a tiny photograph inside, black-and-white, a younger version of my mom and a man with my nose, my chin. Her head is on his shoulder and he's beaming like he's the luckiest man on earth. "It hurt too much to look at all the time, so I kept it in his room. In a jewelry box, on the top shelf of his closet. But it was sitting on my pillow. Did you . . . did you find it? Did you put it here?"

But even as I'm shaking my head we both know who did it. "He wants to tell you something, Mom," I whisper. "Probably goodbye, but maybe something else." I don't try to guess what. That's between my mom, my dad, and my uncle.

She nods and sits heavily on her bed, staring at the locket. I hug her, tell her I'm going to sleep, and that I'll teach her about ghosts in the morning.

Epilogue

Uncle Roderick and I are by the creek. It's a sunny day, and we're having a picnic. My old baby blanket, tattered into a rag years ago, is suddenly a wide and plush quilt spread out across the dreamscape. I'm eating cotton candy; it tastes like stars and clouds and rain. Uncle Roderick is eating from a jar of pickled okra. The sun is hot, making my eyes squint. I can't see him clearly—he keeps flickering in and out of my vision. But I know he's smiling.

"You did it, Bug."

"What did I do?"

"Figured it out. Figured yourself out."

"You helped." I look down at my body. My legs are strong. My arms are toned and tanned. My chest is flat, my shorts sit easily around my waist.

"I wish I could help more. You have the rest of your life to live with this. I don't. But I wish I could tell you."

"Tell me what?"

"How to be. How to be yourself. How to embrace the trials. How to use the triumphs. How to fight and play and win and lose."

"You got me this far. I'd have to find out for myself anyway."
I still can't open my eyes all the way, but the taste of rain is still
sweet on my tongue. I feel arms around me and I know it's Uncle
Roderick hugging me.

"Thank you," I tell him. He kisses me on the cheek. The tightness of his embrace fades away. His middle name was Thomas,
I remember. Tommy. That's a good name. I can live with that.

Author's note

Your friend: "Ooh, that book looks good! What's it about?"

You, maybe: "It's a ghost story! It's about a kid named Bug, her uncle—I mean, his uncle—uh, wait, so, their uncle—um."

If you're having a hard time figuring out how to refer to Bug, or Tommy, and how to talk about his story, that's okay. I'm not always sure how to talk about it either!

When people talk about my childhood, I want them to refer to me as he: "When Kyle was little his family lived in Chicago," even though when we lived in Chicago everyone still thought I was a girl, even me. Most trans people I know want to be talked about the same way. But Bug doesn't know that about himself, for most of this book, so it's also okay that people in the story are calling him "she" and "her."

But if you've just finished this book, and want to tell your friend to read it, you probably don't want to call Bug she/her, because you know better. But referring to Bug as he/him might feel like taking away your friend's chance to fully experience the story.

Here's what I do: When people ask what my book is about, I say, "It's about a kid being haunted by the ghost of their dead uncle into figuring out something important!" Bug never uses they/them pronouns, but I hope that if I say it quickly enough, the person I'm talking to won't really notice. If the person asks for more details I might say that it's kind of a scary story, and also a sad story but with a mostly happy ending, and that it's about figuring out how to make friends, being who you are, and letting go of someone you love.

If you're talking about the book with a friend who's also read it, of course you can call Bug he/him the whole time (and I hope you do). But I also trust you to describe it to someone who hasn't read it yet, in whatever way feels right to you, so long as you hold the truth of who Bug is in your heart. Thank you for joining him along the way.

Acknowledgments

When I was a kid, my dad told me about a story he once wrote. He didn't remember much, but was proud of the first sentence: "It was strange living in the old house, now that Uncle Roderick was dead." Thanks, Dad, for a great opener. And Mom, for understanding my bookish ways.

For eight years I was the librarian at Corlears, which taught me everything I could ever want to know about writing for kids. Thanks to my students, who brought immeasurable value, and a lot of writing ideas, into my life. And to my colleagues (especially Amy-Marie, Lindsay, Sam, Dora, Chelsea, Patricia, Alex, Joy, and Charles), who modeled treating children with respect. One morning I told Ellen Vandenberg that I didn't know what to write first, a trans middle-grade novel or a ghost story using my dad's opening line. The answer: "Why not both?" My roots go down.

In 2014 I sent Saba Sulaiman fifty pages of a manuscript. She thought I wasn't there yet as a writer, but encouraged me to keep working, and reach out if I felt ready. In 2019 she fell in love with Bug and his old house and it's been an agent/writer match made in heaven ever since.

My editor, Ellen Cormier, has been a dream to work with (and even sends me cute cat pics). Thank you, and the whole team at Dial Books, for making so many of my dreams come true.

Friends and community: Seven Boudin, whose childhood home inspired the setting, Jax Jackson, Robbin, Riley MacLeod, Meredith Russo, Heidi Heilig, Tobi, Zev Alexander, Vee Signorelli, Alex Gino, my platonic boyfriends Gaines & Mike & Ben, Susannah Goldstein, Karyn Silverman, Kate Sullivan, Emily Dobbins, Traci Sorell, Eric Alger, T'ai Chu-Richardson, Angie Manfredi, and every trans guy I've shared community with, whether we like each other or not.

I wrote most of this book at Outpost Cafe (z"l), on the traditional land of the Lenape people.